VOICE OF
AMERICA

C.1

VOICE OF AMERICA

STORIES

E. C. Osondu

HARPER

An Imprint of HarperCollins*Publishers*
www.harpercollins.com

HarperCollins books may be purchased for educational, business, or sales promotional use. For information, please write: Special Markets Department, HarperCollins Publishers, 10 East 53rd Street, New York, NY 10022.

Many thanks to the fine publications in which these stories first appeared: *Agni, Vice Magazine, Fiction, Stone Canoe, Skive, Guernica, New Statesman, Atlantic, Weaverbird Collection*, and *Kenyon Review*.

FIRST EDITION

Designed by Renato Stanisic

Library of Congress Cataloging-in-Publication Data
Osondu, E. C.
    Voice of America : stories / E.C. Osondu. — 1st ed.
        p.   cm.
    ISBN 978-0-06-199086-1
    I. Title.
PR9387.9.O856V65 2010
823'.914—dc22
                                                    2010005729

10   11   12   13   14   ID/RRD   10   9   8   7   6   5   4   3   2   1

Warmly and affectionately dedicated to the memory
of my mother, Kadi Beatrice Osondu

Contents

Waiting

My name is Orlando Zaki. Orlando is taken from Orlando, Florida, which is what is written on the T-shirt given to me by the Red Cross. Zaki is the name of the town where I was found and from which I was brought to this refugee camp. My friends in the camp are known by the inscriptions written on their T-shirts. Acapulco wears a T-shirt with the inscription "Acapulco." Sexy's T-shirt has the inscription "Tell Me I'm Sexy." Paris's T-shirt says "See Paris and Die." When she is coming toward me, I close my eyes because I don't want to die. Even when you get a new T-shirt, your old name stays with you. Paris just got a new T-shirt that says "Ask Me About Jesus," but we still call her Paris and we are not asking her about anybody. There was a girl in the camp once whose T-shirt said "Got Milk?" She threw the T-shirt away because some of the boys in the camp were always pressing her breasts forcefully to see if they had milk. You cannot know what will be written on your T-shirt. We struggle and fight for them and count ourselves lucky that we get anything at all. Take Lousy, for instance; his T-shirt says "My Dad

Went to Yellowstone and Got Me This Lousy T-Shirt." He cannot fight, so he's not been able to get another one and has been wearing the same T-shirt since he came to the camp. Though what is written on it is now faded, the name has stuck. Some people are lucky: London had a T-shirt that said "London" and is now in London. He's been adopted by a family over there. Maybe I will find a family in Orlando, Florida, that will adopt me.

Sister Nora is the one who told me to start writing this book—she says, "The best way to forget is to remember, and the best way to remember is to forget." That is the way Sister Nora talks, in a roundabout way. I think because she is a Reverend Sister she likes to speak in parables like Jesus. She is the one who has been giving me books to read. She says I have a gift for telling stories. This is why she thinks I will become a writer one day.

The first book she gave me to read was *Waiting for Godot*. She says the people in the book are waiting for God to come and help them. Here in the camp, we wait and wait and then wait some more. It is the only thing we do. We wait for the food trucks to come and then we form a straight line and then we wait a few minutes for the line to scatter, then we wait for the fight to begin, and then we fight and struggle and bite and kick and curse and tear and grab and run. And then we begin to watch the road and wait to see if the water trucks are coming, we watch for the dust trail, and then we go and fetch our containers and start waiting and then the trucks come and the first few containers are filled and the fight and struggle and tearing and scratching begin because someone has whispered to someone that the water tanker was only half full. That is, if we are lucky and the water tanker comes; oftentimes, we just bring out our containers and start waiting and praying for rain to fall.

Today we are waiting for the photographer to come and take our pictures. The pictures that the Red Cross people send to their people abroad who in turn show them to different people in foreign countries. After looking at the pictures, the foreign families will choose those they like to come and live with them. This is the third week we have been waiting for the photographer, but he has to pass through the war zone so he may not even make it today. After he's taken the photographs, we have to wait for him to print them and bring them back. We then give them to the Red Cross people and start waiting for a response from abroad.

I want to go and join my friend under the only tree still standing in the camp. Acapulco is raising a handful of red dust into the air to test for breeze; the air is stagnant, and the red earth falls back in a straight line.

"Orlando, do you think the photographer will come today?" he asks.

"Maybe he will come."

"Do you think an American family will adopt me?"

"Maybe, if you are lucky."

"Will they find a cure for my bedwetting?"

"There is a tablet for every sickness in America."

"I am not sick, I only wet myself in my sleep because I always dream that I am urinating outside and then I wake up and my shorts are wet. I think it was only a dream, but the piss is real."

"The same dream every night?"

"Yes."

"Do you think that if I go to America, my parents will hear about me and write to me and I will write to them and tell my new family to let them come over and join me?"

"When the war ends, your parents will find you."

"When will the war end?"

"I don't know, but it will end soon."

"If the war will end soon, why are the Red Cross people sending us to America?"

"Because they don't want us to join the Youth Brigade and shoot and kill and rape and loot and burn and steal and destroy and fight to the finish and die and not go to school."

Sister Nora says it is good to ask questions, that if you ask questions you will never get lost. Acapulco begins to throw the sand up once more, testing for a breeze. Pus is coming out of his ears, and this gives him the smell of an egg that is a little rotten. This was another reason people kept away from him. A fly is buzzing around his ear; he ignores it for some time, and at the exact moment the fly is about to perch, he waves it away furiously.

"I wish I had a dog," he said.

"What do you want to do with the dog?"

"I will pose with the dog in my photograph that they are sending to America because white people love dogs."

"But they also like people."

"Yes, but they like people who like dogs."

"London did not take a picture with a dog."

"Yes, London is now in London."

"Maybe you will soon be in Acapulco," I said, laughing.

"Where is Acapulco?"

"They have a big ocean there, it is blue and beautiful."

"I don't like the ocean, I don't know how to swim, I want to go to America."

"Everyone in America knows how to swim; all the houses have swimming pools."

"I will like to swim in a swimming pool, not the ocean. I hear swimming pool water is sweet and clean and blue and is good for the skin."

We are silent. We can hear the sound of the aluminum sheets with which the houses are built. They make an angry popping noise like pin-sized bullets. The houses built with tarpaulins and plastic sheets are fluttering in the breeze like a thousand plastic kites. Acapulco raises a handful of dust in the air. The breeze carries it away. Some of it blows into our faces, and Acapulco smiles.

"God is not asleep," he says. I say nothing.

"There used to be dogs here in the camp." He had been in the camp before me. He was one of the oldest people in the camp.

There were lots of black dogs. They were our friends, they were our protectors. Even though food was scarce, the dogs never went hungry. The women would call them whenever a child squatted down to shit and the dogs would come running. They would wait for the child to finish and lick the child's buttocks clean before they ate the shit. People threw them scraps of food. The dogs were useful in other ways too. In those days, the enemy still used to raid the camp frequently. We would bury ourselves in a hole and the dogs would gather leaves and other stuff and spread it atop the hole where we hid. The enemy would pass by the hole and not know we were hiding there.

But there was a time the Red Cross people could not bring food to the camp for two weeks because the enemy would not let their plane land. We were so hungry we killed a few of the dogs and used them to make pepper soup. A few days later, the Red Cross people were let through and food came. The dogs were a bit wary, but they seemed to understand it was not our fault.

And then, for the second time there was no food for a very long time. We were only able to catch some of the dogs this time. Some of them ran away as we approached, but we still caught some and cooked and ate them. After that we did not see the dogs again; the ones that ran away kept off. One day, a little child was squatting and having a shit. When the mother looked up, half a dozen of the dogs that had disappeared emerged from nowhere and attacked the little child. While the mother screamed, they tore the child to pieces and fled with parts of the child's body dangling between their jaws. Some of the men began to lay ambush for the dogs and killed a few of them. They say the dogs had become as tough as lions. We don't see the dogs anymore. People say it is the war.

I decided I was going to ask Sister Nora. As if reading my mind, Acapulco told me not to mention it to anyone. He said people in the camp did not like talking about the dogs.

"I am not sure the photographer will still come today," I said.

"Sometimes I think there is a bullet lodged in my brain," Acapulco said.

"If you had a bullet in your brain, you would be dead."

"It went in through my bad ear. I hear explosions in my head, bullets popping, voices screaming, '*Banza*, *banza* bastard, come out, we will drink your blood today,' and then I smell carbide, gunsmoke, burning thatch. I don't like smelling smoke from fires when the women are cooking with firewood; it makes the bullets in my brain begin to go off."

"You will be fine when you get to America. They don't cook with firewood; they use electricity."

"You know everything, Zaki. How do you know all these things though you have never been to these places?"

"I read a lot of books—books contain a lot of information. Sometimes they tell stories too," I say.

"I don't like books without pictures; I like books with big, beautiful, colorful pictures."

"Not all books have pictures. Only books for children have pictures."

"I am tired of taking pictures and sending them abroad to families that don't want me; almost all the people I came to the camp with have found families and are now living abroad. One of my friends sent me a letter from a place called Dakota. Why has no family adopted me, do you think they don't like my face?"

"It is luck; you have not found your luck yet."

"Sometimes I want to join the Youth Brigade, but I am afraid; they say they give them *we-we* to smoke, and they drink blood and swear an oath to have no mercy on any soul, including their parents."

"Sister Nora will be angry with you if she hears you talking like that. You know she is doing her best for us, and the Red Cross people too, they are trying to get a family for you."

"That place called Dakota must be full of rocks."

"Why do you say that?"

"Just from the way it sounds, like many giant pieces of rock falling on each other."

"I'd like to go to that place with angels."

"You mean Los Angeles."

"They killed most of my people who could not pronounce the name of the rebel leader properly, they said we could not say 'Tsofo,' we kept saying 'Tofo' and they kept shooting us. My friend here in the camp taught me to say 'Tsofo,' he said I should say it like there is sand in my mouth. Like there is gravel on my tongue. Now I can say it either way." Acapulco passed his tongue over his dried lips as he said this. His eyes looked a bit wet.

"That's good. When you get to America, you will learn to speak like them. You will try to swallow your tongue with every word, you will say *larer, berrer, merre, ferre, herrer.*"

"We should go. It is getting to lunchtime."

"I don't have the power to fight. Whenever it is time for food, I get scared. If only my mother was here, then I would not be displaced. She would be cooking for me; I wouldn't have to fight to eat all the time."

We both looked up at the smoke curling upward from shacks where some of the women were cooking *dawa.* You could tell the people who had mothers because smoke always rose from their shacks in the afternoon. I wondered if Acapulco and I had yet to find people to adopt us because we were displaced, we did not have families. Most of the people who have gone abroad are people with families. I did not mention this to Acapulco; I did not want him to start thinking of his parents, who could not say "Tsofo." I had once heard someone in the camp say that if God wanted us to say "Tsofo," he would have given us tongues that could say "Tsofo."

"Come with me, I will help you fight for food," I say to Acapulco.

"You don't need to fight, Orlando. All the other kids respect you, they say you are not afraid of anybody or anything and they say Sister Nora likes you and they say you have a book where you record all the bad, bad things that people do and you give it to Sister Nora to read and when you are both reading the book both of you will be shaking your heads and laughing like *amariya* and *ango*, like husband and wife."

We stood up and started walking toward the corrugated sheet shack where we got our lunch. I could smell the *dawa*, it was always the same *dawa*, and the same greenbottle flies and the same bent and half-crumpled aluminum plates, and yet we still fought over it.

Kimono saw me first and began to call out to me; he was soon joined by Aruba and Jerusalem and Lousy and I'm Loving It and Majorca and the rest. Chief Cook was standing in front of the plates of *dawa* and green soup. She had that look on her face, the face of a man about to witness two beautiful women totally disgrace themselves by fighting and stripping themselves naked over him. She wagged her finger at us and said, "No fighting today, boys." That was the signal we needed to go at it; we dove. *Dawa* and soup spilling on the floor. Some people tried to shove some into their mouth as they fought for a plate, in case they did not get anything to eat at the end of the fight. I grabbed a lump of *dawa*, tossed it to Acapulco, and made for a plate of soup, but as my fingers grabbed it, Lousy kicked it away and the soup poured on the floor. He laughed his crazy hyena laugh and hissed, "The leper may not know how to milk a cow, but he sure knows how to spill the milk in the pail." Chief Cook kept screaming, "Hey, no fighting, one by one, form a line, the *dawa* is enough to go round." I managed to grab a half-spilled plate of soup and began to weave my way out as I signaled to Acapulco to head out. We squatted behind the food shack and began dipping our fingers into the food, driving away large flies with our free hands. We had two hard lumps of *dawa* and very little soup. I ate a few handfuls and wiped my hands on my shorts, leaving the rest for Acapulco. He was having a hard time driving away the flies from his bad ear and from the plate of food, and he thanked me with his eyes.

I remembered a book Sister Nora once gave me to read about a poor boy living in England in the olden days who asked for more from his chief cook. From the picture of the boy in the book, he did not look so poor to me. The boys in the book all wore coats and caps, and they were even served. We had to fight, and if you asked the chief cook for more, she would point at the lumps of *dawa* and the spilled soup on the floor and say we loved to waste food. I once spoke to Sister Nora about the food and fights, but she said she did not want to get involved. It was the first time I had seen her refuse to find a solution to any problem. She explained that she did not work for the Red Cross and was their guest like me.

I was wondering how to get away from Acapulco—I needed some time alone, but I did not want to hurt his feelings. I told him to take the plates back to the food shack. We did not need to wash them because we had already licked them clean with our tongues.

As Acapulco walked to the food shack with the plates, I slipped away quietly.

Bar Beach Show

The year I turned thirteen, my father took me and my elder brother, Yemi, to Lagos's Bar Beach to witness the death by firing squad of the notorious armed robber Lawrence "The Law" Anini and his gang of seven robbers. A few years later my brother Yemi was also to die by firing squad as an armed robber.

Anini and his gang had held Lagos hostage for over three months, so much so that the head of state had asked the inspector general of police on national television how soon the robber was going to be arrested.

We did not hate The Law; he did not bother us. He only stole from the very rich and from the banks. On one occasion when the police were after him and his gang, he had torn open a bag of naira currency notes and flung fistful after fistful into the air. There had been a stampede as the people on the street ran into the road to pick up the money. In the ensuing melee, he had escaped with his gang, and the next day the *Lagos Daily Times* ran the headline "The Law Beats Police Once Again."

My mother objected to our going to witness the shooting of

the robbers, but my father paid her no heed. He told her that these days some robbers were as young as twelve, and that he wanted us to see with our eyes what happened to those who did not obey the laws of the land.

"Did you not see the ten-year-old boy nicknamed Smallie who was shown on television the other night? The robbers said he was the one who crawled in through the air conditioner chute into most of the homes they robbed. They said he ran away from the Lagos Remand Home at six and was a hardened marijuana smoker."

"But think of all that blood, Baba Yemi. I don't think it is something that the children should see. There are other means you could use to persuade them. Besides, the beach is usually filled with people smoking and drinking on execution days."

My mother said this while looking at me and my brother Yemi for support, but none was forthcoming. I was looking forward to attending the executions. My friend in school who had attended one told me there were *suya* sellers hawking barbecued meat on sticks and itinerant *bata* drummers drumming for a gift of pennies. I was not about to miss this because of Mama's squeamishness and misgivings. My brother Yemi was silent as usual. He was busy polishing his sandals. First he applied very little polish to the sandal's leather surface; then he took it out beyond the concrete steps to dry in the sun. He then brought it back indoors and began rubbing the leather tenderly with a piece of clean rag. Dad had once remarked that if only Yemi paid as much attention to his books as he paid to polishing his sandals, he would come out tops in his class.

The Lagos Bar Beach, which was formerly named Victoria Beach in honor of Queen Victoria of England, had lots of myths surrounding it. It was said that once every seven years a large animal that was neither fish nor fowl was cast on the beach by the furious waters of the Atlantic. A crowd would gather from the length and breadth of Lagos armed with knives and baskets to get a piece of meat for their cooking pots. The most amazing thing, according to those who had witnessed this event, was that no matter how much each person cut, there was always enough for the next person. This was why the meat was called the inexhaustible Bar Beach meat. It was said that just as mysteriously as the animal had appeared, the inhabitants of the city would wake up one morning to discover the big animal had disappeared.

It was also said that a beautiful mermaid would lie naked on this beach every full moon during the seventh month of the year and admire its own beauty as reflected on the water, that whoever was lucky enough to see the mermaid naked could ask for anything that he wished for and his desire would be granted. It was said that the mermaid called Mamiwata was the one that gave a guitar to the legendary guitarist Sir Victor Uwaifo.

We were going to the beach in Dad's brown Lada car. It was still new then. That was before he was retrenched in the confectionary factory where he worked and began to use the car for *kabukabu,* ferrying baskets of decaying tomatoes and half-rotten yams from distant places for market women. Dad was wearing his favorite milk-colored French suit, and his hair was dyed and neatly combed. He was pointing out different places to Yemi as he drove, but Yemi was as surly as an unhappy dog and only twisted his handkerchief around his fingers.

"This road used to be the only road that ran through Lagos. It was narrower than this then, and very few cars plied it." He turned to Yemi, leaning his neck back, his eyes darting to the road in front and back to look at him.

"Even back then, CMS Grammar School was already in existence. It is the oldest school in Lagos; that was why I was so happy when you got in."

Yemi was silent. I was embarrassed for Dad, but Yemi was always making me feel this way. Creating big silences never embarrassed him. Street hawkers were poking cones of ice cream and multicolored candy sticks into the open window of the car for us to buy, but Yemi only glared at them.

"That used to be Fela's former house and nightclub; it was burned down by soldiers from Abalti barracks," Yemi said to me. It was the only time anything had excited him since we left the house. He was interested in music and was learning to play the guitar, which was a sore point between him and Dad.

"You cannot fight the government—he was harboring miscreants in his club, and his girls were smoking marijuana and moving around half naked all over the street. He should have known that you cannot challenge soldiers and get away with it," Dad says.

"He was fighting for the people with his music," Yemi insisted. "The soldiers threw down his mother from a six-story building, which was what led to her death."

"A stubborn child always brings disgrace and sorrow to his parents. This is why I keep telling you children to always listen to me and your mother because we want the best for you." Dad said this in a tone that suggested the argument would go no further.

Yemi became silent again and only stared into the lagoon that we were driving past, from which a decayed smell of shit and garbage wafted into our nostrils.

We could hardly find a place to park the car as we approached the Bar Beach. There was a large crowd of people on foot walking toward the beach. There were hawkers carrying plastic buckets filled with block ice and soft drinks, screaming, "Buy cold minerals, cold 7 Up, and Pepsi here."

Dad took my hand and Yemi's hand, but Yemi snatched his hand away and made to walk ahead of us. Dad shouted at him to stay close to us.

The robbers were already tied to tall metal drums buried in the sand by the time we got to the beach. They were tied so tightly the blue nylon rope was cutting into their skin. Their leader, Lawrence Anini, was puffing a cigarette. He held the cigarette with his teeth because his hands were tied by his side and blew out the smoke through his nostrils and one side of his mouth. Sweat was running down his face, which looked ashen, as if coated with a thin film of powder. He was wearing a deep frown. As the cigarette burned down and he spat it away into the sand, people began to scramble to pick up the cigarette butt. A police guard picked it up, pinched dead the burning end, and put it in his pocket. I heard someone in the crowd say that the cigarette was a good luck charm; he said anything from the body of a dead man was powerful, but Dad only sniffed.

Soon the soldiers who were to carry out the execution arrived in an olive green truck. Policemen wielding horsewhips created space within the crowd, and the soldiers began to take crouching positions before the robbers. A woman screamed that someone had snatched her purse, which led to a discussion among some people in the crowd.

"Can you imagine? In a place like this somebody is stealing. You know the best thing for thieves is just to shoot them like this *gabadaya*."

"I hear The Law's native doctor is somewhere around, casting spells and mouthing incantations so that no bullet can penetrate his body," someone in the crowd said.

"I heard he shot and killed his native doctor some time ago so that she cannot prepare the same *juju* she made for him for someone else."

"Let them start, I want to see their blood flow, we shall see today whether it is not the same red blood that flows in the veins of law-abiding citizens that flows in theirs."

"Ah, look, one of them is crying like a baby already; look at the crocodile tears, the way they are flowing out of his eyes."

One of the robbers, his name was Victor Osunbor, was actually crying. He was said to be the best shot of all the robbers and could shoot accurately while steering their getaway car with one hand. His teardrops mixed with the sweat that was running down his face and the mucus from his nose, turning his face into a dark slippery mess.

"Most robbers, especially the hardened ones, will always weep before their execution; they want you to pity them but they themselves have no single pity in them," Dad said to a man who was standing beside us. The man was tugging at his little beard, and his eyes darted from one side of the crowd to the other.

"Oh yes, they always weep. I have seen all of them weep, from Oyenusi to Omopupa to The Boyisgood to Shina Rambo, all the robbers that have been shot here at Bar Beach, the strong ones are the ones who weep most."

"They do not deserve any pity. I know that if they are released now the very next night they will return to the only job they can do well—robbery. Don't you agree?" Dad said, turning to the man, who had gone back to tugging at his beard.

"Yes, oh robbers deserve to die, no mercy at all is what I believe in fact this new military government should allow us to stone them to death like they do in Saudi Arabia, I swear to God if they let us stone them, I will pick up the heaviest piece of stone in this Bar Beach and smash it *gbosa* on their heads," the man said, smiling, his bloodshot eyes glinting.

Yemi was talking with one of the itinerant musicians who were working the crowd. For a little penny you could request a song that they would sing for you while strumming on their guitar. Yemi was telling the musician to play him a rock number by AC/DC, but the musician laughed and told Yemi that he did not play such songs, that they were not popular and were hardly requested. Yemi asked to borrow the man's guitar, but the man refused, telling Yemi that he was looking for money right now and was busy. As the man moved away, Dad turned to Yemi and smiled in a dry way.

"You see now for yourself how a so-called musician is no better than a beggar, look at all of them in their uncombed hair and unwashed jeans begging for pennies from everybody, after this how can you still want to be a musician?"

"Is it not better to beg with your guitar than to become an armed robber?" Yemi responded. Dad opened his mouth to say something, but closed it and began to mop his face with his damp handkerchief.

"Aha, they will soon start," the man beside us said. "The Reverend Father and the Imam are both here now." A priest was walking from one of the men at the stake to the next and whispering into their ears. He spent a long time with Victor Osunbor, who was heaving dry sobs. The priest gave him rosary beads, which he quickly wrapped around his fingers, and began to make signs of the cross on his forehead and chest.

The leader of the soldiers, a warrant officer, blew his whistle. "Take your positions," he bellowed. "Get ready. Fire! Fire! Fire!" he screamed. As the shots rang out, the crowd screamed.

Suddenly it began to rain. Fat dollops of rain were cascading from the open skies, drenching everyone quickly and making people turn to each other with accusatory looks. The rain washed away the pool of blood that gathered by the executed men. Men wearing yellow overalls with the inscription "Lagos Island Local Government" began untying the bodies and throwing them into the back of an open tipper lorry.

A debate had broken out among the crowd as the people dispersed. Some people among them said the rain symbolized something. The man with the darting eyes said to Dad that The Law was a great man for rain to have fallen on the day he died, but Dad hissed, "No, not at all. The rain is cleaning away everything, sweeping away their memory so that the country can be clean once again."

"Rain only falls when important people die, like when kings die it rains. The Law was the king of robbers; that is why it is raining," the man said, looking around triumphantly.

Dad took us by the hand, and we began to walk toward his car. Just as the rain had started, it suddenly stopped. Humid vapors rose from the beach as we walked toward the car. We drove to the ice cream stand of Leventis Stores, and Dad got us some Wall's ice cream and Gala sausage rolls. I ate my ice cream halfway and dozed off. When I woke up, we were home, and my melted ice cream had formed a banana-colored puddle on the car's floormat. Yemi had finished his and was chewing the flat stick that had held the ice cream.

The newspapers reported that later that night some people

went to the unmarked graves where the robbers were buried at Atan Cemetery and cut their chests open and removed their hearts. They said that they used them to prepare powerful charms that would make them fearless.

We came back from school one day and saw Dad holding a piece of paper and supporting his head on his hand. Mama was sitting beside him and occasionally muttered, "You must take heart and be strong. It is not the end of the world; when one road closes another will open."

"This is the handiwork of my enemies," Dad said. "They have been praying for my downfall, and now they have succeeded, the enemies have done their worst, what am I going to do?"

"What about the other people who were retrenched? I thought you said there were others that were laid off too?"

"Yes, they said it is the government's austerity measure that has made everything so difficult. But why me? There are so many other people that were asked to go, what did I do? I am always the first person to get to the factory, and now . . . who is going to pay the children's school fees and the rent and our feeding?"

"I will leave for the village soon to go and start doing some little farming and trading. At least that will be bringing in a little something, and you can start some business with the little money you were paid."

Mama left for her ancestral village. She had extended family there. We only heard from her once in a very long while. Dad began to dabble in different businesses that left him with less and less money. I recall one that had to do with the production of emery paper, but nothing came out of it. What I remember was that for a long time the corridor that led to my room was piled high with cartons of the stuff. Dad had tried selling it to the local welders and motor mechanics, but they told him the quality was poor. Meanwhile the man who had gone into the business with him had disappeared. Other ventures followed that involved Dad coming up with the start-up money, and sometimes there was a lot of activity and buying of materials and then nothing. This went on for a long time, till Dad was left with nothing and began to use his car as an unlicensed, unpainted taxi at night.

One day I came back from school and saw one of Yemi's teachers who lived down the road from us talking with Dad. He told Dad that Yemi had stopped attending classes and had been placed on suspension twice. He said Yemi had been running with a gang that hung out on Pepple Street, where Fela now had his new nightclub. He told Dad that he had heard that some of the boys carried miniature axes and locally made pistols in their schoolbags.

When Yemi came in that night, Dad screamed at him, calling him a shameless and ungrateful son who was working hard at spoiling the family's good name. And then Dad relented and began to plead with Yemi to have pity on him and not to allow himself to be contaminated by bad boys.

The next morning when we woke up, Yemi had gone from his room, taking a few clothes and his beloved pair of sandals with him. He did not forget to take along his LPs by Fela. When I told Dad that Yemi had left, he cursed him and swore that Yemi was no longer his son.

Occasionally on my way to school I would see Yemi on the street corner with some tough-looking boys, smoking marijuana. He would wave to me and give me a crumpled ten-naira note. One day one of his friends extended the marijuana to me, but Yemi got very angry and snatched it from him and threw it into the black stinking open drain beside us.

A few months later I came back from school and met a policeman from the Panti police station waiting for Dad. He told Dad that Yemi had been arrested for armed robbery and was awaiting trial with the members of his gang. He said that a member of their gang had informed Yemi and the other members of the gang that his sister was visiting the country from America and that she had come back with lots of dollars. In the course of the robbery the boy had called out to a member of his gang to hurry up, and his sister, who was lying facedown on the floor, had recognized his voice and had screamed and torn away the mask from his face. The leader of the gang had shot her, and they had fled. The police later tracked them to their hideout and arrested them. Dad listened to the policeman and for a long time did not speak; then, pointing at me, he said to the policeman, "This is the only son I have, my other son died many years ago."

Yemi was later executed at the Lagos Bar Beach with other members of the gang. For a week I did not go to school and Dad did not drive his taxi, and when I returned to school, people would point at me on my way to school and whisper.

Our First American

The first American we really got to know up close was a guy called Mark. He lived on our street with a prostitute named Beauty. She was what we called a club girl. She visited various Lagos nightclubs to drink and dance with men and would go home with any who offered her enough money. Sometimes the men would drop her off in the mornings. On other occasions a motorcycle taxi would drop her off at the street entrance. She would enter the street through the smaller pedestrian entrance, clutching her bag in one hand and her high-heeled shoes in the other. She would stop over at the neighborhood corner shop to buy cigarettes. You could tell from the way she walked into the street whether she had had a successful night or not. She either walked in with a swagger, her buttocks swishing, or on bad days came in with drooping shoulders. On days that her night had not been good, she tore into Mark as soon as he opened the door of their one-room apartment.

"You this useless American man, simply to get up from the bed and open the door is too much for you, look at how long I have been knocking, eh, and I have been out all night searching for what you and I will eat."

"Honey, I am sorry, I didn't hear you."

"Don't honey me; you have been sleeping while I have been going all over Lagos from Lido to Scala to Kakadu Night Club looking for business, just look at me, I am all bones because of you."

"Take it easy, my baby."

"Who is your baby, eh, please, I am not your baby, if I was your baby you will take care of me the way other big Americans who live in big mansions in Lagos take care of their girlfriends. Or do you think I don't want to sit at the owner's corner of an air-conditioned Mercedes Benz and give orders to my personal driver to take me round the big department stores and the jewelry and clothes shops?"

"Hey, baby, come on, calm down, you are pretty upset this morning, huh?" Mark would say lightly, and laugh.

"Laugh at me, laugh, it is not your fault. It is my fault for taking you into my house when the bank sacked you, all the small girls you were fucking up and down when you were working at the bank, where are they today? Eh, tell me where are they? If not for me, Beauty, you will be sleeping under the bridge like a common street boy. I don't blame you; it is my bad luck that I blame! All my friends who are doing this type of my business, they have all married their American boyfriends and left for Kuwait, Venezuela, and Houston. Here I am still suffering to feed you in this one room."

"Come, baby, let me roll you some real good grass, it will help you step down."

We would hear them light up, and the smell of marijuana and

incense would float out of their room like the Harmattan haze. A few minutes later we would hear them making love very loudly.

The men on the street with dirty towels tied round their waists and holding toothbrushes and cups of water pretending to be brushing their teeth, who had all the while been listening and enjoying the exchange, then would launch into a discussion about the lovers.

"White people know how to love their women, *jare*. If it is our own people, he would have taught her a lesson with a few strong slaps and kicks, but I hear that white people, once they are in love, they are in love. They don't believe in marrying many wives like we do."

"It is true, my brother, I worked with one of them, Engineer Kennedy, when I was a driver with Exxon Mobil, before I was retrenched. Him and the wife, they were always kissing, every minute they kissed, when the man was going to work they kissed, when he returned from work they kissed again, after eating they kissed, and they were kissing right before my very two eyes. And do you know they had no children? The woman had a small white dog that sat on her lap from morning till night like her baby while she smoked long American cigarettes."

"Someone told me that Mark used to work with a bank but was sacked because he spent all his time with club girls and would go to work late after drinking through the night. Sometimes he would not come to work at all. I hear the bank sacked him because he was running up huge tabs in the nightclubs, and club girls would come to look for him in the bank and would sit in the banking hall with their heavily made-up faces, smoking cigarettes."

"Just imagine a white man living with a club girl on this, our dirty street," one of them said. "All the white people I know, they live in big houses in the European quarters. The streets there are well paved, and they don't suffer power outages like we do here. The street names in the part of Lagos where they live are beautiful: McIver, McPherson, Bourdillon, Boygues, not like our own streets that have rough-sounding names like Ajangbadi, Okokomaiko, and Dadakoada."

"But why can't the man find a job? He is not like us, he should be able to get another job, the white people like themselves, they are not like us, who do not like anyone who is not of our tribe."

The men would talk till they got tired. One of them would then bring up the story they had heard on the radio about a politician caught in London with bags of stolen state funds. Once again the conversation would become animated. At this point one of them would recall that he had somewhere important to go, and the men would then disperse.

At about midday we saw Beauty going to the corner store to buy some bottles of beer and packets of pasta. She swayed her hips from side to side; the men looked at her and scratched their jaws while the women looked away and hissed. She came back to the house and brought out her cassette player and her stove and began to prepare her pasta sauce. She was dancing to the music from the radio as she cooked. It was the music of Afrobeat legend Fela Kuti—one of his more obscene songs, in which he sings about what a man and a woman do behind closed doors and how their six-spring bed creaks noisily. Her neighbors blocked the ears of their children with their fingers and dragged them into their rooms. Mark sat on a low bench, rolling a marijuana cigarette while reading a fat novel. His hands were stained a dark brown from the marijuana. Beauty was dancing for him.

Twice she snatched the book from his hands while telling him to watch a sexy sway she was executing. It was said that white people did not like pepper in their food, but Mark was an exception. He ate the same spicy foods that we ate and would on occasion go with a bowl to the roadside food vendor, Mamaput. The people on the street said that any white man who eats pepper would never leave Lagos. This seemed to be true for Mark.

And then one day, Beauty threw out Mark's things. She was coming back from down the road where she had gone to buy marijuana when she saw Mark talking with a girl who lived on the same street. Her name was Bridget, and she was an undergraduate at the University of Lagos. They had been discussing one of the novels Mark was reading. He was always reading fat books that were sold cheaply on Lagos sidewalks. They were still talking when Beauty stumbled on them. She pulled up her trousers, clapped her hands, and screamed, "Come and see this small girl prostitute husband snatcher that wants to take my man."

"Come on, Beauty, we were only talking about books," Mark said, trying to placate her.

"You shut up your dirty mouth there, I will face you later, let me finish with this small *ashewo* first! So you and your mother have been planning on how you will steal my man, you people are no longer satisfied with calling me names behind my back and whispering when I pass, you have shown your hands, me, I will show you people today."

She grabbed Bridget by the front of her dress and tore the dress, exposing her breasts. The girl began to cry. People in the compound came out and forcefully pried her hands off the girl, but not before she had left a bleeding mark with her nails on the girl's face.

She went inside the room and started throwing out Mark's things, beginning with his cheap paperback novels and his sneakers and his faded New York Yankees baseball cap and his faded jeans and his checkerboard. She dumped them outside, screaming while she tossed them out, cursing her neighbors for being backbiters, husband snatchers, witches, and wizards.

Some of the people who had lived on the street for a long time swore that Mark was going to come back. They said they had seen it happen so many times in the past, and Mark always came back in the middle of the night.

Not too long after that, we saw Mark on television and on movie posters. When Beauty threw Mark out, he had gone to a popular hangout for artistes near the National Theatre called Abe Igi to see if he could locate some old friends from his banking days who drank there. An actor informed Mark that a movie producer who specialized in shooting quick movies with video cameras that were sold in Lagos traffic was looking for a white man to play the role of a colonial missionary in an upcoming movie titled *The Cross and the Pagans*. Prior to this time, the filmmakers had cast albinos wearing wigs in the roles of white men. This time, they wanted to use a real white person. Though Mark had no formal training as an actor, he got the role and played it well. The producers of the movie invested a lot of money promoting the movie on radio and television and also plastered every available space on major streets with posters.

That same week Beauty walked into the street brandishing the movie poster with Mark's photo on it. She slapped her thighs and held up the poster.

"Was it not you people of this street that said my man was an idler? Come and see him now, he has become James Bond, go to

Scala Cinema tomorrow and see my man in action. Those of you who are rejoicing that he has left me, our love is still strong, let me tell you, he will walk back to me with his two legs."

People on the street pretended not to be listening, but we were all ears. Some of the men and women were making comments in whispers.

"Some women have bad luck," a woman called Sisi Yellow because of her skin color said. "They will suffer with a man for a long time *so tey*, but as soon as they tell themselves they cannot take the suffering anymore and move out of his house, the man's luck changes. When I was living on the other side at Ajangbadi it happened to a woman I knew. She had seven children and was drinking *garri* and wearing the same brown cloth every day, but the day after she left her husband, he won five hundred thousand naira from Face-to-Face Pools."

"Beauty may be lucky; the man loves her. White people's love is forever. Once they love, they love."

"Not in this case. Do not forget she threw the man out *gaba-daya*, she even tossed his slippers out, and in our culture it means she no longer wants to see his two legs in the house. And she also swept her house after he left; it means she is done with him."

"That will be too bad, I mean after all they went through together. Remember the time the man nearly died of typhoid fever right before our eyes, and she could not afford to take him to the hospital, and he was drinking boiled traditional roots and herbs?"

"The man is not going to remember that. Men do not remember the good that women did for them. But do one bad thing to them, and they will not forget it, that is what they will be saying each time you quarrel."

Beauty must have overheard some of the comments because she began to sing a popular Fuji song, "Let my enemies live long and see what I will become in future."

The film was a success. It was so successful the cast toured the entire country. The film was shown in schools and was commended by the military head of state as a great work with cultural authenticity.

Beauty told people on the street that Mark was going to come back to her when he returned from his tour. She even said he had sent her a message through another actor.

The tour ended, and Mark did not return. We heard he was on location shooting another film on the slave trade and was playing the role of the evil and notorious slave dealer Captain Wilberforce Bomberbilly. It was also said that he had commenced a relationship with an actress and had even moved in with her.

Beauty told anyone that cared to listen that Mark visited her in her dreams every night and had reassured her that he was coming back for her with gifts of gold and lace and high-heeled shoes. Her business was not going too well either, because each time she met a man at the nightclub, she began to tell him about her white boyfriend turned popular actor Mark. Her stories made the men yawn, and the other girls began spreading rumors that she had lost her mind. This was after they saw her standing alone in the dark talking aloud to herself: "Come to me, my lover, why did you leave me, come let me show my new style of bedmatics, come to me, my lover. I have always known you will come back to me." A few of the girls laughed at her, but one of them went to her, took her by the hand, and led her back to her house.

One morning she came back with a taxi and crammed her things inside, cursed out everybody on the street as witches, wizards, wasters, rumormongers, bad luck people, and gossipers. And then she left and never came back again.

As for Mark, he actually married the actress and took her to America, but we heard they got divorced after a few months. Mark came back. People on the street said they were not surprised. Any white man that eats pepper must return to Lagos.

Jimmy Carter's Eyes

When she was three, the girl accidentally upturned the boiling pan with which her mother was frying bean cakes on herself. The hot oil left two thick lumps of scar tissue across her eyes, blinding her. Her mother had told everyone who came to sympathize with her that she believed that a nurse had said they'd cut off the scar tissue in the hospital and the girl would be able to see again. Actually, she had been told this not by a real nurse but by a doll-baby nurse. This was the name given to auxiliary nurses in the general hospital where she had stayed with the child for three months, watching the eyes covered by gauze and gentian violet.

No one blamed her for what happened to the child. No women in the village spent all their days watching their children. A woman had thousands of chores—fetching water and firewood, washing clothes, cooking for the family—and looking after the children somehow fitted itself around these activities. She had left the child by the boiling oil and had run inside to fetch her salt container. She needed to sprinkle a pinch of salt into the boiling oil to know if it was time to dunk the ground beans into it. By the time she ran back out, the little girl had grabbed the boiling pan of oil. She screamed, and a crowd gathered quickly. As is traditional in the village when such things happen, many took a look at the child and ran back to their homes to bring different medications, some useful but most useless. Some came with an expired bottle of gentian violet, another came with a smelly black bottle filled with the fat from the boa constrictor killed five years back. One came with a lump of wet cassava that she said would cool the skin and leave no scars. All these were dumped on the girl's face. Someone screamed for the midwife. The Mid ran the village dispensary. She did more than deliver babies: she wrote prescriptions, sold drugs, and gave injections. Mid took a look at the child and ordered that she be taken to the general hospital in the local government headquarters, which was a good ten miles away. A commercial motorcycle taxi was called, and the woman, holding the child close to her, rode away to the hospital. The crowd gathered around the fire, which had grown cold, and began to talk about the incident.

"It is always money, money, money for the young women nowadays. In my time this would not have happened."

"It was not her fault. She has to take care of herself and the baby. You know her husband simply woke up one morning and walked away."

"I have seen worse burns in my time. She is young, and the skin will heal very nicely. You'll be shocked when you see the same child many years hence. There will be no single blemish on her skin."

"My boa oil can heal anything. They need not have taken her to the hospital—just a drop of the oil on the burn every morning and she would heal perfectly."

"Oh, the oil from the boa constrictor that was killed years back, I remember it was so big people thought it was a log of wood that had fallen across the road. From the black marks on its back you could tell it had lived for close to forty years."

"I have a bottle of the oil myself. I simply forgot to bring it."

"I wonder why Mid told her to take the child to the general hospital. With the different medications we have applied, even if the skin was burned by the fires of purgatory she should heal."

"You know she is the eyes and ears of the government among us here. Her job is more than giving babies with running stomach salt and sugar solution to drink. They sent her here to speak as the voice of the government. If you disobey her, you could get into trouble."

"You know, since she got here, the tax collectors now know the best days to come, they now come on days when everyone is at home. Who do you think tells them?"

People in the crowd looked at each other as if they had spoken too much and began to disperse. Toward evening, the driver of the motorcycle taxi came to tell the woman's neighbors that she had asked that they bring a few of her clothes to the hospital. She also told them to search under her sleeping mat and bring all the money there to the hospital.

The people in the village gathered and drew up a roster of people who would take food to her in the hospital. Some volunteered to go pass a night with her in the hospital but were told not to bother by the woman. The hospitals were overcrowded, and families of patients slept on the open veranda of the hospital. Those who had gone to the hospital said the place stank of carbolic acid and death. They said that because of frequent power outages, the ice melted from the bodies of the corpses in the mortuary and the corpses stank like decomposed frozen mackerel. They said the doctors and nurses had their own private clinics and preferred that patients came to consult them there rather than in the general hospital. They said the child's eyes were covered with gauze and that she could not swallow and had to be fed through a straw.

The woman and her daughter stayed in the hospital for a long time. Longer than people stayed in the hospital when they went to have their hernias removed. No one followed the roster anymore; the villagers became busy with planting their crops. Another woman began to fry *akara* by the roadside, and people began to buy from her. Occasionally people spoke of the woman and her daughter and then looked away embarrassedly.

One day the woman returned with the little girl, who had by now grown a bit. Two thick layers of scar tissue now covered the girl's eyes. She was blind, which was rather odd. A blind little girl was unheard of. In the village, people became blind when they grew old. They said everyone chooses the part of his body that would age more than the other parts. Some chose their ears and became deaf as they grew old. Others chose to age in their teeth and lost all of them.

The girl's mother smiled and did not say much. She did not complain that she had been abandoned in the hospital. She soon went back to her business of frying *akara* by the side of the road. There was no animosity between her and the other woman who had also started frying *akara*. She said the sky was wide enough for many birds to roam without their wings touching each other.

The child sat by her mother and would sometimes pass salt and other items to her. The mother would leave her to go into the house, and people would come and buy *akara* and the girl would collect their money and give them the correct change. This was very strange because the girl had not been to school, and even if she had, she was blind, so how could she distinguish between one currency note and another?

One day a little girl went missing in the village. Sometimes children would go missing, but they would normally be found within a few hours. This was different. Many hours had passed and the girl was still missing. When a child went missing, the mother of the child would tie her headscarf tightly around her waist and go around the village crying and asking, "Who has seen my child?" It was generally believed that by the time she lost her voice, the missing child would be found. By the second day the child was still missing. Even though the mother had lost her voice, the child was not yet found. When the mother walked past the women frying bean cakes, crying and screaming, "Who has seen my child?" the blind girl spoke for the first time.

"I know who stole the missing girl."

"Be quiet and don't get us both into trouble."

"I saw him give the girl a piece of candy; he tied her mouth with a rag, and threw her into a jute bag and rode away on his motorcycle."

The woman had never heard the child say that many words. Whenever the child chose to speak, she spoke in a whisper. Many people assumed she never spoke at all.

The mother called out to the woman. She said out loud what the child had said. The villagers gathered. There was only one man they knew who rode a motorcycle and had a jute bag: the man who bought cocoa beans from the villagers. They sent some young men after him. They caught him with the child two towns away. He had cut a hole in the bag through which he fed the girl. He had kidnapped the child for juju moneymaking rituals. It was rumored that little virgin girls could be charmed and made to vomit money through juju. He cried and said the devil made him do it.

The parents of the kidnapped girl brought a gift for the blind girl and her mother. There was no attempt to explain how the girl had arrived at the knowledge she had. Some people said she must have heard something. They said her blindness had sharpened her ears. Her mother suspected something but said nothing.

One day the girl said softly to the mother, "Father is never coming back."

"Why do you say that? I am not sure you remember your father, you were so tiny when he left."

"He ran away with the catechist's wife's younger sister."

"How do you know that?" the woman asked, puzzled and frightened.

"They were traveling to Mokwa. He was going to start a new life with her. The car in which they were traveling broke down on the way; all the passengers came down while the driver opened the bonnet to find out what was wrong. He was crossing to the other side of the road to urinate, when a car coming from the other side knocked him down."

"Oh, my child, how do you know these things?" the woman asked.

"They buried him by the roadside, his grave is overgrown with weeds, he's never coming back."

The woman was quiet for a while. Everything about the story sounded true. She began to cry quietly to herself.

All things eventually come to light. People in the village sensed the girl's true powers and began to come to her for answers.

"Will there be plenty of rain this year so I can plant cassava instead of yams?"

"My black sheep did not come home with the rest of my sheep last night. Where could it be?"

"My son who lives in the city has not come home for five years. Is he dead or in prison?"

"My son who died three years ago: Was his death a natural death, or did my husband's other wife poison him while I was out of the house?"

"Is the price of cocoa going to rise or fall this year?"

"My husband has been sick for years now; do you think he will recover?"

The girl answered all their questions in a whisper, and she answered honestly. Her answers occasionally caused trouble, tore families apart. Her mother would sometimes speak to her by way of signs to be quiet, but she spoke up all the time. The answers flowed out of her mouth like a gentle stream. She said what she had to say and was quiet.

Prosperity began to come to the village because of her. People planted the right crops at the right time and got very rich harvests. Evil was rare. People stopped stealing because they knew she would find them out. More farmers bought motorcycles. Life had never been better.

The mother stopped frying *akara*. She made a comfortable living from the gifts the girl received. She was happy for once in all her life. She always felt the girl's eyes on her and sometimes shivered slightly when she felt the girl was looking at her. The girl's voice did not change, her breasts were small. The mother was happy when she began to bleed in tiny drops every month. *Thank goodness she is a woman*, she said to herself.

People said different things about the source of her power, but no one denied it.

"Her power is from the river goddess. When she speaks, it is the river goddess speaking."

"It is the Holy Virgin that gives people such gifts, that is why she is called the voice of the dumb and the eyes of the sightless."

"She is not Catholic, not even Christian—she does not mention the name of God."

"God who took away her eyes gave her the gift of sight, and now she sees more than those of us with two eyes."

People said all sorts of things but still came to her for answers. On occasion the mother would say the girl was tired and needed to rest, but the girl would come out of her room and provide answers to whomever needed them. People reminded the mother that she could now afford to take the child to the Baptist Missionary Hospital in the big city. The mother acted as if she did not hear them. She did not think it was wise to tamper with the will of God, she told those who were bold enough to ask her. Besides, if the girl thought it was such a good thing she would have said so. Quite a few agreed with the mother; after all, those of them who were not blind did not see as much as the girl did.

At about this time, the former American president Jimmy Carter launched his River Blindness Eradication Program. The program sent doctors and nurses to villages to distribute drugs for the prevention of river blindness. They did eye examinations and distributed glasses, which the villagers referred to as Anya Jimmy Carter—Jimmy Carter's Eyes. The frames of the glasses were secondhand, gifts and donations from affluent Americans. This time around, though, it was going to be slightly different;

they were coming with eye surgeons to help remove cataracts. The bearer of this piece of news was the midwife. She told the villagers that she had made it happen, that the village was not originally in the plan for the cataract surgery; she had lobbied for them to be included.

People were excited about this piece of good news. One of the old men in the village said the former president was kind because he had been a groundnut farmer before he became a president. Most of the villagers were farmers.

The doctors had already been to the nearby village and had sent a notice to the chiefs that they were coming. The midwife said they would be moving from house to house.

At first everyone looked forward to the visit, until the woman mentioned that this would be an opportunity for her daughter to have the scar tissue covering her eyes removed. It was free, and the girl was bleeding; she was now a woman and needed to get married. She only said this to a few people. It soon got round the village that the girl was going to undergo surgery. There was anger, there were complaints, there was resentment, and then people began to complain loudly.

"This program is not for people like her, it is for people losing their sight to river blindness."

"She lost her eyes due to her mother's carelessness. Her mother should bear the cost of her surgery in a proper hospital."

"What guarantee is there that she will see again? Even if the skin is lifted, I hear the eyeballs are dead and blank. Please, no one should make the poor child suffer for nothing."

"They say her mother wants a husband for the girl. I know many men that will gladly marry her the way she is, she is a bag of wealth."

"It is the mother that needs a husband. Why did she never re-marry after her husband ran away? As we all know the husband is dead, the girl said it herself."

"The girl belongs to the entire village now, not to her mother alone. She ceased being the mother's property as soon as she received her gift."

"You are right, you know—if the gift was for her alone, she would have stopped at telling her mother about her father's disappearance."

"You are right, she sees things for everyone, she was sent to prosper the village."

"Why are the Americans sending the eye doctors to us? Do they mean to tell us they have cured all the blind people in America?"

"The elders should meet and tell the woman what to do, just in case she does not know."

Words got to the ears of the elders, and they, being people who acted in the interest of the inhabitants of the village, decided to prevail on the mother of the girl to do the right thing. They made their points—they told her that her daughter's gift was for the good of all, that if it was for her mother alone she would have been seeing things for the mother alone. They spoke to the woman for a very long time. The woman told them that the girl was already bleeding and was a woman. She wanted her to marry and have children. Mid came along with the elders. She explained the difference between a cataract and the girl's condition. It was very possible that the girl would not recover her sight after the surgery; this might traumatize the girl, and she might even lose the gift of speech, which would be a double tragedy.

They talked to the woman for a long time. The elders told her that they would gladly marry the girl off to any of their sons. She cried, and then she nodded and agreed with them.

On the day the American eye doctors came, the woman and her daughter locked their doors and remained inside till the eye doctors left. Some people got new glasses; some had surgery. Everyone was happy. The girl and her mother were referred to as heroes who had put the interest of the town above their own interest.

When the planting season began, people came to the girl with their questions, but alas, she had no answers. The stream had dried up.

"It was not our fault. We should not blame ourselves for it," one of the villagers said.

"Whatever has a beginning must have an end; even the deepest ocean has a bottom. She was bound to stop seeing things one day anyway."

"It is the white man's strong juju that did it, or don't you know that white people are powerful?"

"The blind girl and her mother should consider themselves lucky—if it were in some other village, they would have stoned them to death for possessing witchery powers."

And so life returned to normal in the village, and everybody's conscience was at peace. Occasionally when a sheep went missing, the owner would be heard to bite his fingers and mutter, "If only that blind girl still had her powers."

A Letter from Home

M y Dear Son,

Why have you not been sending money through Western Union like other good Nigerian children in America do? You have also not visited home. Have you married a white woman? Do not forget that I have already found a wife for you. Her name is Ngozi. Her parents are good Christians and her mother belongs to the Catholic Women's League like me. Please do not spoil the good relationship I have built over the years with Ngozi's family.

I beg of you not to become like Kaka's son who was sent to America with the community's funds, only to come back with a white woman, and would not let his parents visit him in his white man's living quarters in the Lagos government reserved area. He has large dogs and his white wife treats the dogs like her children. The only time he visited his family, he refused to sleep in his father's old house, complaining that it was dirty, and took his wife to pass the night in a hotel. He stretched out his hands to shake the hands of the elders of the community and would not prostrate on the ground like a well-brought-up child.

Or don't you consider Ngozi beautiful enough from the picture I sent to you of her dressed in a long gown, holding a hibiscus flower? She attended the Catholic Women's Teacher's College and comes from a lineage of women who bear strong sons.

Ogaga's son who went to Germany only a few years ago has sent his father a big black BMW and has already completed a twenty-room mansion and is laying the foundation for a hotel. I am already in the evening of my days and want to rock my grandchildren on my tired knees before I go to heaven to live in the many mansions that God has prepared for me. I have become the laughingstock of the village because I sold my only stall in Oyingbo Market to raise money to send you, my only son, to America, and now I have no stall in the market and am forced to hawk my wares on a tray like a housemaid.

Remember your promise to buy me a car and get me a driver, so I can proudly sit in the owner's corner like the wife of a top civil servant.

I am sure you remember Obi's daughter. She went to Italy to work as a prostitute after you left for America. Just last year she came back with lots of goodies for her parents and has even married a boy from a responsible family. They had their wedding in the church and the priest said that though her sins were like scarlet she has been washed clean by the blood of Jesus (after she made a huge donation for the repair of the church roof). She has gone on to bear a son and now nobody remembers that she was once a prostitute in Italy.

Do you associate with other Africans so you can still

remember your roots? Do you still find African foods to eat? Because I fear the white man's food will make you reason in the white man's ways. My son, reconsider your ways and retrace your steps like the prodigal son, so I can bless you before I die.

I spent too much sending Ngozi to the fattening room. I sent her there at my own expense so the women can teach her the ways to take care of her husband, and feed her, and fatten her up so she can be plump like a ripe melon. God forbid that a girl from a responsible family, like Ngozi, should be looking like dry *bonga* fish on her wedding day. Sending a bride-to-be to the fattening room costs a lot of money these days, because the women who run them are dying out and the younger generation consider it "bush." The young prefer their women thin and dry like broomsticks. They seem not to know that men prefer to hold something ample when they reach out at night.

My son, do not make me a laughingstock. I beg of you not to let those who borrowed chewing sticks from me end up with brighter teeth and cleaner breath. I am sure you remember Odili's son (you were in primary school together). He used to be the neighborhood rascal who smoked marijuana and pinched young girls on their buttocks, and can you imagine, that *efulefu*, that idler, woke up one day and announced that he was going to Europe by road! We all thought that marijuana had finally crossed two wires in his brain, but how wrong we were. He joined a truck carrying tomatoes to the north and boarded a bus from there to Mali, where he joined a caravan of camels across the Sahara desert. Some of those he was traveling with died of thirst in the desert, but he survived. He found work in a construction site in Morocco and saved enough money to pay the Tuaregs, who helped him to cross by boat into Spain. He told the Spanish authorities he was a Liberian fleeing the Liberian war and was given a work permit. You should have been there the day he came back exactly five years later: he was loaded down with television sets, gold and trinkets, clothes, and lots of money, which he spent like water. For the few days that he was around, his father's house was the place to be; it was where everyone went to eat and drink. In my heart I did not want to go there with the throng, but I did not want to be accused of not wishing him well. So I dragged my feet there and ate and drank and rejoiced with the family like everyone else. All eyes there upon me, and asking, "What about your son, when will he return with goodies, when will he invite us to come and eat and drink like the Odilis have done? You whose son flew to America. Look at Odili's son who went on foot, he has come back with goodies." Not that anyone said a word to me, but I could see it in their eyes. Their eyes never left me as I drank the Coca-Cola, and ate *jollof* rice and fried beef and danced foolishly like a headless chicken. The young man has gone back, by air this time, promising his father that when next he comes, he will demolish his father's old house, and put up a mansion in its place.

I have been tempted to give your young bride Ngozi to your younger cousin Azuka so she can produce a baby for me to rock on my knees before they become too rusty. But Ngozi's mother will not hear of it. She clapped her hands cynically and hissed like a snake and asked if her daughter was now a piece of beef on the butcher's table that people tossed and weighed and tossed aside for the next person. She spat derisively at me, narrowly missing my face, and told me that if her daughter was going to marry again, she would look for a better family for her, a family where things grow and not an arid one like ours. Since that incident, she has stopped attending the meetings of the Catholic Women's League and hisses and crosses over to the other side of the street whenever she sees me coming toward her.

You really have no excuse for not sending money, because Western Union now has an office on our street. Daily, I see men and women who have caring children in America marching majestically into their offices and swaggering out with huge bundles of naira notes in large paper parcels. They wave with their free hands and clutch their parcels of money as if afraid I'm going to ask them to lend me some.

Do not imagine that my ears are not filled with all manner of suggestions from different people. After all, as our people say, "The day an elephant dies is the day you see all kinds of knives." A native doctor once suggested to me that he could cast a spell on you over there in America that would make you abandon whatever you were doing and board the next flight back to Nigeria. He said the spell was so effective that even if there was no flight, you would board the nearest boat and return home. But you are my son, you came into this world from between my legs, and I will not do something that will harm you. Okolosi's son was forced back from America by such a spell. He is back home now; he wears an old jacket and walks up and down the street frightening children on their way to school with his hyena laugh while reciting aloud to himself the names of the capital cities of America.

I am not threatening you, but please do not force my hand. You were born the year the Americans landed on the moon and returned with that strange eye disease called *Apollo*. I still remember everyone's eyes turning red and dripping water like a tap as soon as the men came back from the moon. It was said that the disease was God's punishment to the people of the earth for peering too closely into his eyes and leaving an imprint of their feet on his face. It did not surprise me, therefore, when you said you were leaving for America to study. Even as a little boy watching *Bonanza* on our old black-and-white television, you were always taking on new names every week. One week you were Dan Blocker, Purnell Roberts the next, down to Michael Landon and Lorne Green. As a child you would wear a cowboy hat, put a dry piece of wood in your mouth, pretending it was a cigar, curl your lips, and speak through your nose like the actors on television. It did not surprise me when you said you were leaving for America, because you were born the year the American flag was planted on the moon. During moonlight play, while other children saw the man in the moon, you always ran back home to tell me that you saw the American flag waving to you.

And now I want to share a family secret with you. In the early 1940s your father secured a place at Howard University. Your grandfather sold his entire rubber plantation to the United African Company to raise the funds for your father's boat trip via the Elder Dempster Lines. Your grandmother sold her gold ornaments too. When your father got to the Lagos wharf, he fell into the hands of con men, who convinced him they could double his money. The con men were soldiers of the West African Frontier Force, recently discharged from the army after fighting in Burma. They spent their days idling around the wharf looking for gullible bumpkins like your father. Your father reasoned that if they doubled his money he could send half back to his family and travel with the other half to America. The con men collected his money and handed a black wooden box to him, telling him not to open it till the next day. On opening it, he discovered it was filled with neat rows of newspapers cut to the size of pound notes. He was distraught and was about to throw himself into the Atlantic when a woman selling bean cakes by the wharf stopped him and took him home. He got a teaching job in a private school and managed to save enough money to travel to Sierra Leone in search of better opportunities. His family back home assumed he was studying in America. He was in Sierra Leone when his father, your grandfather, became sick. As the first son, he was expected to be there to lay his father's hands across his chest when he breathed his last. The elders conferred and decided to consult a medicine man to cast a spell on your father to bring him back home. It was this spell that brought your dad back from Sierra Leone. By the time he arrived, your grandfather had breathed his last, but not before placing a curse on his son who had broken his heart. He said that just as your father had disappointed him, your father's own children would in turn do the same to him.

Do you still recall the birds that migrated all the way from Australia to our village to nestle in the rice farms? They wore shiny gold bangles around their feet, embossed with the words "Melbourne Zoological Gardens." You must remember going to watch them play and sing all day, as they pecked at rice seeds and bathed in the pools of water by the rice paddies. They were large colorful birds with feathers that looked as if they had been painted with a hand brush. The farmers didn't bother them; they looked like royal visitors and behaved as such, never being overly destructive, unlike the local *kwela* birds, and only pecked at the rice seeds that fell on the ground. As soon as it was time to harvest the rice, they gathered themselves together, conferred for a few minutes as if praying for journey mercies for the trip ahead, and flew off together as a group.

But one year, one of the visiting birds stayed back. While the other birds gathered together, limbering up, preparing for takeoff, it sat on the ground pecking without concern. The departing birds made signs at it and spoke to it in their shrieking bird language, but it did not pay them any heed. Discouraged, the other birds left it behind. When the farmers came the next day, they tried to drive it away and persuade it with signs to fly away and return to its homeland, but it just stayed there pecking at rice seeds. After some time, it flew slowly toward a group of local *kwela* birds and joined them in their destructive scattering of the unharvested rice. The farmers said to themselves that the bird no longer comported itself like a visitor, and decided to do to it what they did to the local birds. They shot it with an arrow and used its meat to prepare rice stew. My son, I hope you have not become like that strange Australian bird that forgot its homeland.

Janjaweed Wife

When we were living in Fur, whenever my sister Nur and I did something Mother disliked, she would frighten us by invoking the name of the Janjaweed. If we whispered to ourselves in the dark as we lay on our mat at night—our same mat that smelled faintly of urine no matter how often it was put out in the sun to dry—her harsh whisper would carry into our room.

"Are you girls not going to sleep? You had better stop your whispering lest the Janjaweed hear you and carry you away on their horses and make you their wives."

Nur and I would laugh quietly to ourselves in the dark and stop our whispering. Shortly Nur would startle me with her wall-shaking snores. I would prod her on the ribs with my elbow. The snores would temporarily cease and then start again, and I would prod her once more. I would prod and prod her and would not know when I fell asleep.

I recall one occasion when Nur was chasing me around the house. We were screaming and laughing and making so much noise, Mother shouted at us to stop.

"Have you people forgotten that you are girls? Good girls do not run around screeching, feet pounding *gidim, gidim, gidim* like the hooves of Janjaweed horses. Both of you had better go and sit down quietly in some corner before I marry you off to some Janjaweed so you can spend all your lives brewing tea."

Nur turned to me and said, "I do not mind brewing tea. It sounds much easier compared to gathering firewood and all the grinding and pounding of sorghum and corn on mortar and the unending trips to the water well that we have to do every day."

"God forbid," I said. "How can you say that, or don't you know that the Janjaweed are djinns riding on horses, and if they pick you as their wife, any day you do not brew their tea fast enough they will pluck out and eat your heart like wicked djinns are wont to do?"

"You have never seen a Janjaweed with your two eyes—or have you?"

"No, but that is because they are spirits, and spirits are invisible. The day you see one you will suddenly grow giant goose bumps, catch cold, and begin to shiver. Your teeth will start to chatter, and then you die and become a spirit yourself."

"God forbid," Nur said to me, her voice quivering. I thought I saw little goose bumps on her dark skin and realized that I might have frightened her. I held her hand as we both walked into the house.

We met Father sitting with his head in his hands. When he raised his head, the whites of his eyes looked as if they were covered with a thin film of blood. He looked tired, and his dark face looked even darker. Mama gestured to us with her eyes to go to our room. We ran into our room quickly, crouched behind the door, listened, and tried to hold our breaths at the same time so they would not hear us breathing fast. Father's voice sounded painful like a sore.

"Their cattle trampled our crops. . . . We thought it was a mistake, but they said . . . they called us slaves, sons of dogs. . . . It is the same news from different districts. . . . Shouk, Krindid," he hissed, and was quiet.

THE NIGHT THEY came, I thought I was having one of my malaria dreams. In my "malaria dreams," as Mother called them, I was always being pursued by either someone or something. Sometimes it was a man with a machete, or a big black animal with two heads, or a big, dark, fiery-eyed dog snapping at my heels. Usually at the point in the dream in which the machete was about to cut my head off or the animal with two heads was about to bite off both of my legs, one in each mouth, or when I felt the dog's hot, fetid breath behind my legs, I would rub my eyes and wake up. Mama would be standing in front of me holding a lantern and looking worried and scared and telling me in a kind voice to go back to sleep. This night was different, though. There was fire and pounding of hooves and what appeared to be floating fire and screaming. Mama swept Nur and me into her arms, and Father screamed for us to run behind the house and hide. From the side of my eyes I glimpsed the Janjaweed for the first time. So they were real? They actually had horses, and their horses emitted fire through every pore. Their eyes were the color of fire, and balls of fire flew out of the guns they carried. Everywhere they pointed caught fire. Our faces, our house, turned the color of fire. Father stood in front of the house. I looked at him and saw that he was no longer black; he, too, had become the color of fire. The evil ones were cursing and laughing and speaking in fast Arabic. I could hear the words they spoke: "Throw the dark-skinned slaves in the fire; let the fire lighten their skins; they are no better than firewood."

Mother grabbed us, and we began to run. We were joined by others who were screaming and running. Behind us was Abok's father, who was carrying the family's lone black sheep on his shoulder as he struggled to balance Abok on the same shoulder. I saw him stumble and fall. This would have made me laugh, but I could not laugh. We kept running, and the fire behind us grew smaller and smaller till we saw it no more.

OUR TENTS AT the Zagrawa Refugee Camp looked like the humps of thousands of ocher camels crouching in the sand. We all liked to call them tents, but they were not real tents. Some were merely old rags tied together; others were made of old plastic bags, while a lucky few had real tents constructed with tarpaulins. Children from whose tents smoke rose were jumping around and playing, the smoke an assurance that they would soon have something to eat. Tents like ours from which no smoke rose filled with the sullen faces of those of us waiting for our mothers to come back from where they had gone to look for firewood. Nur and I would always watch the road for dust rising into the air, our sign to go get our buckets and water basins and go form a line and wait. Sometimes we were lucky to be among the early ones in the line, because after the first few people, the line would scatter. I was happy that the wells had dried up. Each time I looked into the well while fetching water, I would usually see Father's head floating around in it. I would close my eyes and continue to fetch the water without looking. I never told Mother; I did not want to add to her worries. Since we had come to the camp, she had thrown silence around her like a black-colored shawl. These days she smiled only with her teeth, unlike in the past when her smile rose from her heart and I could see the three wrinkles on each corner of her eyes.

When there was still water in the well, fighting went on all day as boys and girls struggled to grab the long rope and tie it to their buckets. More water was spilled in the fight over the rope than was fetched. The strong boys helped the girls they admired to fetch water. I remember that it was while standing by the well watching the fights that I first saw Deng. I cannot talk about Deng now.

Mama did not frighten us with the Janjaweed anymore. She did not even want us to mention the word around her. The only time she had been her old self was when we came back from the office to our tent with clothes that were sent to the camp from America. The Red Cross people had made us wait as usual, and then we were told to walk to the bundle of clothes and pick one T-shirt each. Nur picked one with the inscription "I'm Loving It"; I picked one that said "Shake What Ya Mama Gave Ya." It had a drawing of a girl with long hair and large breasts, who was pointing at her breasts and smiling. I was lucky to get a shirt that was my exact size and was very proud to wear it. I was hoping that Deng would see me wearing the shirt.

"Where do you think you are going to with the picture of that half-naked girl with a hump on her chest?" Mama shouted at me. Nur covered her mouth and began to laugh behind her fingers.

"Answer me, or has someone suddenly cut off your tongue?

Or you think because your father is not here, you now have the license to dress like a wayward girl? You better remove that flimsy piece of cloth and return it to wherever you got it from," she said. She walked into the inner tent, where she began to blow on the firewood, her eyes quickly filling with tears, whether from the wood smoke or from her shouting at me I could not really tell.

Nur was still laughing. I turned to her and whispered that I was going to tell Mama that the inscription on her T-shirt said something bad.

"What does it say? How can you say it is saying something bad? Or is it because you love the girl with the hump on her chest?"

"Yours says 'I'm Loving It.' What exactly are you loving? You are loving being with boys, eh?"

Mother's voice called out to us to come to help with the cooking, and we went inside the tent and began to help remove sand and dry leaves from the flour that Mama was using to prepare our evening meal.

That night the moon came out, and all over the camp there was a certain gaiety, just as if we were still in the village. In the adjoining tent, the men sat around listening to the radio. They drew closer to the radio as the crisp, clear voice of the announcer mentioned Darfur. He pronounced it "Da-Four," and this made some of the men laugh. Mama was feeling happy too, and she began to tell us a story.

"It was on a moonlight night like this that your father proved that he was worthy to marry me. He took more lashes than all the young men who came to ask for my hand in marriage and took the lashes without uttering a sound. In those days, before it was banned by the government in Khartoum as barbaric and a form of idol worship, it was the custom of our people that if two young men were interested in marrying a particular girl, they had to prove they were strong enough by going through an endurance test. My father told the young men that they had to prove that they could protect his precious daughter and were strong enough to protect their cattle from wild animals. There was another boy who was asking for my hand as well as your father. They both stepped out that moonlit night, their bodies covered in ashes and wearing nothing but underpants. One of the strongest men in the village was holding a long, camel-hide whip, flexing it from side to side to drive fear into the hearts of the young men. Your father was fearless and was smiling, his white teeth glowing in the moonlight. The drums began to pound, and the other young man—I recall now that his name was Dau—stepped forward, and the man with the whip struck out suddenly on his back. The whip curled around him like a serpent, and the young man flinched. The drums pounded even harder, and the whip continued to descend. It was at the tenth stroke of the whip that Dau cried out and raised both hands in the air. The whipping stopped. Our custom demanded that he should not cry out, and his crying out meant it was over for him.

"Your father stepped forward, and the whipping started. He neither flinched nor cried out but still had the smile on his face. Even on the twenty-fourth stroke, when his back was a mass of huge welts, the smile was still on his face. The whipping stopped and your father was officially declared my husband because he had proved himself capable of protecting me. The other young man, Dau, fled the village shortly after that. He could not bear the shame, and no woman would have agreed to marry him after his disgrace. He left for the big city and later became a rich trader."

When Mother finished her story, there were tears in her eyes, and Nur and I, who would ordinarily laugh at every story, had tears in our eyes too. We went to bed thinking of our father. This was why we were more than surprised at what happened next.

Mother called Nur and me and told us to go with a few people outside the camp to search for firewood. This was a task that Mama herself was usually worried about doing. The Janjaweed patrolled the perimeter fence that surrounded the camp and often would catch girls and ride away with them on their camels into the bush and do bad things to them. Whenever Mother had to go for firewood, she would usually go with a couple of other women and a few males from the camp for protection. We were excited about leaving the camp and went with the group in search of firewood. We were not so lucky, as the wood in the area around the camp was almost all gone. We could have gone farther, but others in the group said some men on camelback had been seen riding into the bush, so we returned to camp. On our way back, Nur pulled me by my dress and began to whisper about Mama.

"Do you know why Mama sent us out of the camp? It is because she was expecting a very important visitor, and she did not want us to see him. I suspect he is very ugly."

"A visitor? Who is this visitor, or has she found a husband for you at last?"

"I think she has found a husband for herself," Nur said, and covered her mouth as she laughed.

"I think she wants to wash her clothes," I said.

"If she wanted to wash her clothes, she would have told us to stay somewhere around the camp. She need not have sent us far away."

Whenever our mother wanted to wash her sole flowing,

multicolored gown, she would tell Nur and me to go outside to play out of modesty. She would wash the cloth and sit naked indoors waiting for it to dry.

As we entered our tent, I smelled the strong scent of the dark green perfume oil—*bint el sudan*. The smell filled the whole of our tent. It came from a fat man with folds all over his body. Every inch of him seemed to be folded in parts: his face, his arms, his cheeks. He had facial hair and a single gold tooth. He spread out his arms as Nur and I entered, and even his palms were creased and folded in many places.

"Welcome back, children. You came back so quickly and with so little wood, greet Hajj, and do I need to tell you to do that? Greet like good children and thank Hajj for all the good things he has brought for us," Mama said, pointing at a rich-looking bundle lying in the tent. Nur looked at me, and I looked at her. If Hajj had not been looking at us so intently through the folds of his apparently delighted eyes, we would have burst into laughter. Mama's new bride manner was hilarious. Nur and I knelt to greet Hajj, but he drew us up toward himself.

"No, no, do not kneel to greet me. The prophet forbids it. You must never kneel in greeting before anybody from today onward."

As he drew me toward him, I felt the folds of his plump-looking fingers graze my buttocks through my thin dress, and I flinched. I looked at Nur, but his other hand was at that very moment accidentally touching her left breast. Mama was looking down on the floor and smiling.

Hajj soon rose from his position. In rising he reminded me of an old camel as different parts of his body heaved and seemed to jiggle.

"El Hajj, thank you for honoring our modest dwellings with your esteemed presence."

"You need not thank me at all, and you need not worry yourself further. I will take you people out of here soon," he said, his hand sweeping through the tent.

El Hajj was a big trader in the town. He already had four wives and many children. One of the gun-carrying men on horseback who rode round the camp had told him about Mother, and he had decided to take her on as something between wife and concubine. He would take us out of the camp, and we could live in a real house once more. Mama, who told us this, was ecstatic and seemed to be out of breath as she told us even more wonderful things about El Hajj. He was indeed a very holy man and had performed the pilgrimage not just once, but four times. The sand that was used to lay the foundation of his house was from the holy land of Mecca. He fasted once every week, unlike many others who waited until the holy month. Beggars from all over the town came to his gates to be fed every day. In short, Hajj was a saint in huge folds of human flesh.

We moved out of the camp to El Hajj's house. Mama was not exactly his wife, and we did not live in the main house but in a small block of two rooms that was perhaps originally built for his servants.

One night a few days later, El Hajj called me to his bedroom. The room was filled with milk-colored curtains. The bed was high and had a gold-colored pole on each of the four corners. He was wearing his djellaba and was sitting on the edge of his bed. He was smiling and drew me toward his huge belly. I was looking at his soft, white palms and the folds around his neck.

As the soft fingers began to poke around me, they no longer felt soft. I felt like someone was poking sharp bicycle spokes into me. Everywhere he touched stung, and I began to cry.

The next day Hajj called Nur to his room, and when she came back her eyes were red.

"Did he do anything to you?" I asked Nur.

"You tell me first. Did he do anything to you?" Nur asked me.

"Should we tell Mama?" Nur asked me, though I had not answered her first question.

"I think we should go back to the camp," I said. I told Nur that I had hinted to Mama that we did not quite like it here because of Hajj, but Mama had responded that Hajj was a kind and religious man, and that he was only helping us to become better Muslims.

"She is like a new bride. She no longer knows what she is doing. I think we should return to the camp," Nur said, agreeing with me. "The elders will always look out for us," she added.

That night, as soon as it got dark, we began heading back to the camp.

When we walked into the camp, a loud ululation went up. "They have come back. They would rather be thin and free than fat but in bondage," the women sang. The elders began shouting prayers and thanking us for bringing honor to the tribe. Food in trays appeared from different tents, and there was dancing and singing as the moon shone on Zagrawa Camp.

Nur looked at me as we ate, and I looked at her. We should be happy, but we were not. Father would have been so proud of us, but what about Mama? All around us men, women, and children ate and danced.

A few days later Mama came to the camp to see us. First she stood by the entrance to the camp and sent for someone to call us. People in the camp began to whisper.

"So she is now too big and important to step foot in the camp, eh?"

"Why would she not feel important? Look at all that fine jewelry around her neck."

"She should remember that she once lived here and was no better than the rest of us."

"Better to live in the poverty of this camp with my dignity intact than to be a kept woman."

The wind must have blown some of their whisperings into Mama's ears, because she began to walk into the camp as we were running out to meet her. She held us, and we hugged. She was crying and wiping the corners of both eyes with her shawl.

"My children, you both left me alone—your own mother that carried both of you for nine months. How could you do such a thing? I spoke with El Hajj. He said it was a misunderstanding. He only wished to draw both of you closer to him, but you misinterpreted his fatherly gesture."

We looked at each other and stared at the dusty earth.

"He is ready to make amends. He says he will give you both some time to grow closer to him."

Once again we stared at the ground.

"I saw your father in a dream."

That got our attention. We both drew closer to her.

"Your father was unhappy in the dream. He turned his face away all the while that he spoke to me. He said the only way he could turn his face back to me was if I brought you all back and we all lived under the same roof. I promised him I would. You know I can't break a promise made to the departed. If I do, I too will die."

We both gasped. We went back to the camp and picked up our few items and returned to El Hajj's house with Mama. As we entered El Hajjs's compound, he waved at us from a distance. He was sitting on his prayer mat. He had a big smile on his face.

"I told your mother that you are good children. It was a misunderstanding. This is your new home. You will both be very happy here just like your mother."

We both shivered, giant goose bumps on our skin, and walked into the house.

Going Back West

I woke up one morning, and Uncle Dele was standing by the upright mirror in our sitting room; he was looking out into the street from the window and smoking a cigarette. My mother was brewing a cup of tea, and my father was sitting in his favorite cushion chair, shaking his legs from side to side.

I had heard of Uncle Dele and seen photographs of him taken in America. In one of the pictures he was wearing a winter jacket, his shoes half hidden by snow, and standing in front of a large maroon-colored car. He had an Afro hairdo and was smiling very broadly. In person, he seemed a little disappointing; he wore a frown and drew impatiently on the cigarette like a bird sucking nectar. As he exhaled the smoke through his nose and mouth, he licked his lips lightly like a child relishing the taste of candy. I was shocked someone was smoking around my mother; she generally did not permit anyone smoking around her. Uncle Dele's imprint was all over the house; the old books he used when in high school were filled with maxims written in his impeccable handwriting— "Life is but a walking shadow," "Without love what is life?"

"Ideas have legs," "Salutation is not love," and so on. All his old books were stored away in a locker in the pantry, and their outer coverings were wrapped with paper torn from old wall calendars to protect them.

"Hey, man, you've grown quite big," he said to me, flicking the butt of his cigarette out of the window and smiling broadly at me. "C'mon, give me a handshake, my man." I shook his hand, and he pumped it vigorously. "Everything and everyone looks so different, it is weird, you know . . ." He trailed off, running his fingers through his thick hair.

"Your tea is ready, Dele," my mother said to him. He turned to her, sat down, took a sip, and smiled broadly.

"Wow, this is exactly the way I remember it, still the best-tasting tea I have ever drunk."

"Stop teasing me, Dele, you cannot tell me that after all the years you have spent in America you still think my tea is the best; you are just teasing an old woman," my mother said, smiling.

"I kid you not; it is still the best tea. I drank my best coffee in America, but your tea is still the best."

My mother smiled and said, "In that case I should go and prepare one of your old favorites—*jollof* rice."

"Awesome," Uncle Dele said, rubbing his hands together.

I had not expected Uncle Dele to sneak back like a thief in the night. I knew he was studying chemical engineering at the Massachusetts Institute of Technology, one of America's top schools, and was going to return one day soon with a foreign degree to pick up a job with one of the new oil companies. I was going to live with him in his well-furnished flat and go to the university like he did.

That night I stood behind the door listening to him conversing with my father in low tones. My father kept clearing his throat as if there were a small pebble stuck there while Uncle Dele responded in bits and dribbles like a faulty tap dripping water.

"So what did you say happened? I have not really listened to you properly. I have been waiting for a quiet moment like this so you can really tell me what happened."

"There was a party in a friend's house and a fight over a *cocoye*, a Puerto Rican girl."

"You mean you were deported from America because of a fight over a girl? I may not have been to America, but I am not an illiterate, you know; please tell me the truth. What really happened?"

"It was either deportation or jail—I chose to be deported rather than go to jail."

"I still do not believe you, Dele. I have been a father to you even more than I have been to my own children; wherever your father, my late brother, is, he knows I have done as much as he would have. I starved and denied myself to send you to America, and yet . . ." And he cleared his throat again. "Did you kill someone?"

Uncle Dele swallowed loudly and did not say a word. There followed a little silence, then Dad spoke again.

"So what is your plan now? I still know a few people in the University of Lagos—maybe you could enroll there and complete your engineering program. They have a good program, I hear. I am doing this because of my late brother, certainly not because of you. You have behaved irresponsibly, and you have disappointed me, but what can I do? You are still my son."

"I am going back to America, I cannot study in this country. I have made a mistake, and the only way I can make things right is by returning to America to complete my studies," Uncle Dele said.

"Do you think I have a money tree in the backyard? Can't

you see that your own younger brothers are growing up too? They have to go to school, and I am not getting any younger. The soldier boys are playing *cha-cha* with the economy, today they remove tariffs on importation, tomorrow they increase tariffs. Life is tough here, Dele. The austerity measures they introduced last year have made life doubly difficult."

"I will only be needing money for my one-way ticket back. I will bear the cost of every other thing, do not worry. I have disappointed you, I know, but I will make up for it," Uncle Dele said and prostrated himself on the floor.

"Stand up—you are my son, and as our people say in one of their proverbs, you do not throw your child to a lion to eat because the child has offended you. I will do the best I can," Dad said.

Uncle Dele was the son of my dad's younger brother. Though I called him Uncle, we were actually cousins. My dad's late brother was a farmer and lived in the village. He had gone to the farm one day with Dele; the farms were usually some distance from the village. As they were working in the farm, the sky suddenly grew dark, and thunderclouds gathered. It appeared a storm was gathering. They began to run to the barn to hide from the storm because they were afraid the storm could make a tree fall on them. Before they got to the barn, there was a sudden bright flash of lightning. Dele later told people that he felt like he had been struck on the face with a live electric wire. Dele fell down senseless. His father was knocked down too. When Dele woke up, the storm had passed. He touched his father, but his father was no longer breathing. His skin had grown very dark, and his body was stretched taut. Dele ran back to the village and called the village elders. They came and took the body back to the village. A distant cousin was sent to notify my father. There was a lot of crying. Dad was stoic. "What has happened has happened and we cannot question God," he said. Dad traveled to the village and saw to the burial arrangements. After the burial, Dele came to live with us. He always came tops in his class; some people in the village said he was brilliant because he had been to the land of the dead and back. Some said the lightning had ignited his brain. When I was still growing up, Uncle Dele won all the prizes in high school quizzes, debates, elocution contests, and dramatic performances.

I WOULD WAKE up most days and see Uncle Dele all dressed, standing by the window, smoking and listening to Jimmy Cliff's "Going Back West" and "Suffering in the Land" and "Vietnam." It was from him I first heard that Americans were fighting in one far-off country called Vietnam. The track he played over and over again, however, was "Going Back West." As Jimmy Cliff sang, he sang along with him, his fingers pointing in a westerly direction. He would drink his tea and leave the house for Lagos Island, where the corporate offices and embassies were located. It was also the location of the criminal enclave nicknamed Oluwole, where people could obtain forged international passports and birth certificates.

One day Uncle Dele came back and told my father that he had made some contact that would take him back to America.

"What kind of contact have you made? You have to be careful—Lagos Island is filled with con men."

"These are not con men. I have made contact with a musical promoter, he is taking King Pago and His Rhythm Dandies on an American tour. He has agreed to take me along as a member of the band for a fee of one hundred thousand naira."

"Are you not going to go through an interview at the embassy?" Dad asked him.

"The interview is just going to be a formality; I will be dressed like the other band boys and will be playing an instrument."

"But you are not a musician, Dele."

"I am practicing how to play the conga drums, I am rehearsing with them already."

"You have not given me enough notice—how do you expect me to raise such a huge amount of money within such a short time?"

"Don't worry about the money. I have already paid half of the money to them and will pay the remainder as soon as we get the visa."

"Oh, I did not know you came back with bags of money," my Dad said, chuckling and sounding relieved.

I began looking forward to Uncle Dele's return to America. He had already promised me that as soon as he got back, he would start sending me the latest clothes and magazines, and as soon as I was done with my secondary school education, he was going to help me get into the Massachusetts Institute of Technology.

Uncle Dele came back from the embassy looking glum. He stood by the window, smoking stick after stick of Benson and Hedges cigarettes and staring into the distance. When Dad came back that evening, I heard them conversing.

"They denied all of us visas."

"I thought you said the arrangement was foolproof, that the interview was a mere formality."

"The consular officials asked us to play for them. We played, and they seemed to be enjoying the music, but they said they could not give us a visa. They said it was wintertime in America, and that our promoter should know that people do not attend outdoor musical shows in wintertime. They said we should reapply in the summer."

"What about the money you paid? Is the promoter going to refund it?"

"He says he will, but don't worry, I am already on to something else. Someone I met at the embassy says there is some other way of getting into America, and he is asking for only fifty thousand naira."

"Dele, you are spending money like water. Like I said before, I can get you into the University of Lagos. In a couple of years you will be done, and then you can get a job with the National Petroleum Corporation and settle down and marry so my late brother's name will not be lost."

Uncle Dele told me of his new scheme to get back to America through the Cayman Islands.

"From the Cayman Islands, America is just a spitting distance. I will get a passport from the island and get into America with it. I will not even need a visa. It is so easy, I wonder why I had not thought of this myself."

"Since it is so easy, maybe I can join you for the trip," I told Uncle Dele.

"No, you don't need to go with me—just read your books, and when your time comes, you will come to America like a prince."

"Thanks, Uncle Dele—I know you will do your best for me, but promise you will not forget me when you go back this time."

"C'mon, my man, you have my promise—now run along and bring your mathematics textbook, and I will teach the easiest way of solving the quadratic equation." He had an easy manner of teaching, and all things became easy as soon as he explained them. We would end our sessions with him smiling and saying to me, "If your teachers ask you whose formula you used to get your answers, tell them it is Uncle Dele's formula."

The trip to America by way of the Cayman Islands did not work for some obscure reason, and Uncle Dele became withdrawn.

One evening, the moneylender's black Peugeot station wagon pulled up in front of our house and parked. The moneylender, who was a potbellied man with a pockmarked face, got out and asked for Uncle Dele. The moneylender's name was Maikudi, and he was known in our neighborhood for his unorthodox ways of getting his money back from debtors. Whenever his car was parked in front of anybody's house, it meant the person's debt was overdue. On his way out, he would be clutching a goat if the money owed was not much; if it was a lot, he went away with a young boy or a young girl, one of the children of his debtor. He had a bakery, a block factory, a poultry farm, and a large cassava and yam farm. He would put the children to work until their parents paid up. He had many wives, and some of them were girls whose parents could not pay what they owed.

My dad came out and greeted him. He offered him a drink, and Maikudi accepted. He drank a glass of the beer and wiped his mouth with the back of his hand and belched in a satisfied manner.

"What brings you to a poor man's house like mine?" my dad said, smiling nervously.

"It is your son Dele I have come to see," Maikudi said, suddenly losing all affability.

"You mean my son who just came back from America?"

"Yes, he is the one I am looking for. We have some unfinished business. In fact, there is no need hiding anything from you; he owes five hundred thousand naira. He promised he was going to send me the money as soon as he returned to America, but that was a long time ago. I came to ask him how he intends to pay. Of course he can always work for me—I am planning to open a petrol filling station."

"Dele, where are you? Come out here," my dad shouted. Uncle Dele shuffled in from his room; he stood before my dad, staring at the floor. Dad looked at him and shook his head.

"Maikudi, take it that I am the one owing you. I will arrange to pay you somehow; you know I am not a rich man, but I will try."

"I trust and respect you. Take your time and pay me any number of times you like. You are not the type who will owe me and make me fret whether you can pay or not." He drank the remainder of his beer and left our house, belching.

After Maikudi's visit, Uncle Dele moved out of our house and moved in with some friends of his who lived in Lagos Island. We hardly heard any news about him, but the little we heard confirmed that he was still working on going back to America. My dad kept saying that he would soon come to his senses and return home and follow his advice to enroll in the University of Lagos.

And then there was a coup, and two frowning generals took over the reins of government. They promulgated a new decree every day and launched what they called the War Against Indiscipline. Anyone caught spitting, urinating, or hawking on the street was arrested by members of the War Against Indiscipline Brigade, tried by a special mobile court, and given a long sentence of fifteen to twenty years. They promulgated a decree making it an offense punishable by death by firing squad to traffic in hard drugs, and made the decree retroactive.

We were watching television one evening and were shocked when we saw Uncle Dele and two other young men in handcuffs on the screen. The newscaster said that they had been caught at the Murtala Muhammed International Airport with many kilograms of a powdery substance suspected to be cocaine while trying to board a KLM flight to America. Mother gasped, and Dad screamed, "This boy has killed himself, oh my God, how am I going to explain to his father when I get to the land of the spirits that I tried my best for him?"

We managed to get a few details from Uncle Dele's friends. They said that in his desperation to return to America, he had hooked up with some drug barons who promised him a visa in return for helping them carry a little parcel of cocaine into America. They assured him that they had contacts both at the Murtala Muhammed Airport and J. F. Kennedy Airport in New York. It was going to be a cakewalk, and besides, they would pay him seven thousand dollars for his efforts. What the drug barons and Uncle Dele did not know was that the previous day, the customs and excise officers at the airport had been changed and replaced by a new set of officers.

Dad made an effort to save Uncle Dele. He got him a very brave young lawyer and worked some of his contacts in the military, but was told that the new rulers had made up their minds to set an example with Uncle Dele and the other two people caught along with him. Dad moved from one newspaper editor to another and begged them to write about the draconian nature of the decree under which Uncle Dele was being tried. The editors were afraid. Some of them had had their offices raided by soldiers, and it was rumored that a new decree was in the works to muzzle the press.

Finally the trial commenced at the Bonny Camp Military

Barracks. When Dad came back on the first day of the trial and Mama asked him how it went, he said it was not looking good at all. The lawyer had told him that he was scared; a source had told him that if he put up too much of a vigorous defense, he would be charged with aiding and abetting the drug pushers. He said Uncle Dele looked scared and sickly and pleaded with Dad to save him, "I do not want to die, I do not want to die, my mind would be a terrible thing to waste, please help me."

Uncle Dele was found guilty of trying to smuggle an illegal substance and sentenced to death by firing squad. He was executed one cold Harmattan morning in Kirikiri maximum-security prison.

After Uncle Dele's death I tried to forget about going to study in America and began preparing for the national university entrance examinations. My mind was not in it, though. I would read the same lines over and over again, and sometimes the words on the page would run together like a stream in front of me. I did very poorly in the exams. My dad was very disappointed, even more so my mother. One day my mother called me into her room and began to question me.

"Why did you not do well in the entrance examinations, eh? Look at all the boys who you have always done better than. Some of them are going into the University of Lagos, even that blockhead Alaba is going into Yaba Polytechnic."

"I can't concentrate, Mama," I said.

"Tell me what is disturbing you—is it Dele?"

"Yes," I said.

I began telling Mama of how I would always see Uncle Dele in a corner of my room with a cigarette dangling from his lips whenever I was studying. On another occasion I had seen the tip of his cigarette glowing in the dark as I made my way to the toilet in the backyard. There was a shocked look on my mother's face. I was looking directly at her face and noticed it had turned a little ashen.

"Was he smiling when you saw him?" my mother asked. She was standing so close to me that I could see the giant goose bumps that had materialized on her skin.

"He looked sad each time I saw him; he would shake his head from side to side and walk away from me."

"Oh, my Maker, help me. And you did not think you should tell either me or your father? That is how he would have taken you with him to the land of the spirits, and my enemies would have had the victory over me."

I think she must have relayed our conversation to my dad, because it was not too long thereafter that Dad began to make contacts with some officials in Kirikiri Prison to have Uncle Dele's body exhumed so that he could be properly buried. Mama told me that she suspected Uncle Dele's spirit was wandering because his life had been cut short, and the only way his spirit could rest was if he was buried properly. On my part, I imagined that it was more likely that even in death, he still wanted to go back to America. Dad had to bribe a lot of people, and they even had to put the decaying bones of another dead prisoner in his grave, as the warden told Dad, "You cannot be too careful with the military boys."

Uncle Dele's partly decomposed body was brought back secretly and buried in the dead of night in a corner of our large compound.

The Men They Married

Ego married a certified nursing assistant who claimed to be a medical doctor. He sent her glossy, smiling pictures of himself in a lab coat. When he came to pay her bride price that December in Lagos, she was the envy of friends and neighbors. Everyone referred to him respectfully as "Doctor." Her parents were very proud of her achievement. She recalled her mother telling her friends that it took a patient fisherman to hook a big fish. Her new husband appeared humble, and people talked about his levelheadedness.

"Imagine, a big medical doctor who worked in one of America's best hospitals coming back to Nigeria to marry a wife," their guests whispered in reverential tones. "He left all the beautiful girls in America and came back home to Nigeria to marry a local girl; now tell me, if that isn't humility, then what is?"

She joined him a few months later in America and discovered that he had not been anywhere near a medical school. He worked at Duyn Home, a retirement home for the elderly. He came back home every day smelling of the aged, and complained about the

ninety-eight-year-old Rose Kelly, who grabbed him by his shirt
each time he tidied her and whispered into his ears, "Tell me
about lions, did you ride a cub like Tarzan back in Africa?"

She did not know how she survived those early days—their
cramped apartment building, where fifty other tenants shared a
common laundry room in the basement; the mice and roaches
in the apartment, the paper-thin walls that separated them from
their neighbor, whose piping voice she heard every night screaming at her partner, "Fuck me like a whore." She felt rage, dis-
appointment, anger, shame, and finally numbness. The kind of
numbness that made everything seem like a dream from which
she would soon wake up, with her husband reassuring her that it
had all been a game devised by him to test her, to find out if she
really loved him. Reassuring her that he was indeed a doctor and
had only been pretending otherwise to see if she loved him for
him and not for his title.

She did not recall at what point she began telling lies to her
folks back in Nigeria about him. "Yes, he is really a doctor,"
she told her mother. "He works in one of the largest and most
respected hospitals in America. He is the only Nigerian working
there. No, he is indeed the only black person working there."
And what about the promises he had made to her parents, the
plot of land he had promised to buy for her father in the old part
of Ikoyi, and the duplex he promised to build for him, facing the
Atlantic Ocean? What about her younger brothers and sisters he
had promised to see through college, what about the car he had
promised to ship to her father as soon as he got back? She had
made excuses. He was attending a course, a specialist course at
Harvard Medical School; as soon as he was done, he would take
care of all the things he had promised to her parents.

Soon, she no longer answered those odd-hour calls that came from Nigeria, calls that did not recognize the six-hour time difference. In time, she too trained as a certified nursing assistant. She called home and told her mother that she too was now in medical school. Her mother clapped and screamed with joy and told her she had made her proud and that she could now meet her maker in peace. How many families in Nigeria had sons-in-law who were doctors married to daughters who would soon qualify as doctors themselves? her mother asked.

UZO MARRIED TWO men. That was the way she phrased it whenever she was talking about her situation to other Nigerian women in Maryland. Her husband already had a seventeen-year-old son from a previous marriage to an African American woman, a seventeen-year-old with the strange name Jequante. Her husband said it was an African name. Her husband had brought the boy to live with them two weeks after she joined him from Nigeria. Jequante was over six feet tall, a footballer with strapping muscles, and she was barely over five feet tall. The boy never called her by name but referred to her as *she*. The boy never said good morning to her. The boy never washed the dishes with which he ate. She had been brought up by her mother to believe that the kitchen was a woman's domain. She had never seen her father enter the kitchen. Jequante would ransack her pot of *ogbono* soup and stew and eat all the fish and meat. He ate ravenously, and when he was not eating he would be in the basement sleeping and letting out huge snores and farts that reverberated through the house. He would be on the phone for hours and would tell those calling to speak with her that she was not home. Of course, never referring to her by name, always saying *she* is not here right now, *she* cannot take your call, *she* stepped out.

Jequante, who she once overheard telling someone on the phone that he was going to kick her ass. When she reported this to her husband, he told her that it was a mere figure of speech, it was the way African Americans spoke. Jequante, who would carry his schoolbag as if he was going off to school and wait till her husband left for work and come back to eat and tie up the phone with unending calls. Jequante, who had been thrown out of a dozen schools and had been warned that if he got thrown out of his present one, it would be his last chance. The same Jequante whose father, her husband, had bought him a bike. He had sold off the bike and used the money to fund his marijuana habit. She had smelled a strange odor coming out of the basement and had walked in to see Jequante finishing the remains of a stick of marijuana. She had stared at him, and he had stared back at her, taking a final drag from the weed and walking past her to the kitchen to pour himself a tall glass of milk, which he drained in one gulp, leaving the glass on the stovetop for her to wash. She could not hide her shock when she told her husband about it later that night. Back in Nigeria, she had been told that marijuana was a leading cause of insanity, and it was smoked largely by motor park touts and street miscreants. Her husband had reassured her that it was no big deal here. He told her marijuana was like cigarettes here in America, that most kids dabbled with it in high school, and that it was not addictive. It was then she realized the explanation for Jequante's huge appetite and unending naps.

Jequante, who began dating a woman twice his age, a woman with a gravelly voice who once called the house and, when Uzo picked up the phone, asked her who she was, and when she told the woman that she should be the one asking her who she was, the woman had angrily dropped the phone. She had reported the incident to her husband, and this was one time she had seen him concerned. He had picked up the phone and called the woman.

"Do you know that boy is just a kid? He is only seventeen," her husband had told the woman on the phone.

The woman had laughingly told her husband, "Jequante ain't no kid, he's a real man, my man."

Her husband had threatened to call the cops and child services, and the woman had told him to go ahead and do whatever he wished to. At that point Jequante had stepped in and told Uzo's husband to leave the lady alone, that she was only a friend, actually, the mother of a friend from school.

Jequante, who she had never seen open a book, who she had never seen doing any homework; the six notebooks in his backpack were as blank and clean and virginal as they had been the day they were bought.

And then one day her husband had pretended to go to work. He wanted to confirm that Jequante was skipping school. He came back after an hour and met Jequante on the phone, smoking a cigarette and watching porn on their cable television. They had screamed at each other. She was in the bedroom when she heard Jequante telling her husband not to lay hands on him. She had heard shoving and grunts and had run downstairs and met them both in the kitchen. There was blood on both of them. Her husband was holding a knife. Oh, my God, he has killed his son, was the thought that ran through her mind. They had left each other, and her husband had called the cops. Actually no one had stabbed the other. Her husband had a boil on his left arm, and it had burst while they were struggling. The cops had advised her husband to send Jequante back to his mother in Texas. In the two weeks after Jequante left, her husband had become morose and would not talk to her. He sat in the basement drinking E&J brandy and hissing and holding his head. She was the one who begged him to bring Jequante back, if that was the only thing that would make him start talking to her again. Jequante would soon be on his way back and she would be married to two men yet again.

EBONE WAS SAID to have given her husband away with her own hands. They had come to America on visitor's visas and had decided to stay on. Her husband had found a job in a gas station with fake papers. She stayed home watching talk shows and daytime soaps and dreaming of a time when she too would begin to wear cashmere sweaters like the women on television. When her husband told her that he could pay someone three thousand dollars to marry him so that he could get a green card, she had told him to go for it. How could she have known that they were both embarking on a journey whose end she did not know? She had not even bothered to ask her husband who the lady in question was, or how they had met. She had trusted him fully as she had always trusted him. When he told her she would need to grant him a divorce so he could marry the other lady, she agreed. He had explained that it was not a real divorce; they would both still be living together. And then he had told her he would need to take a few of his clothes to the lady's house to keep up appearances just in case the Department of Immigration people needed to confirm they were both living as man and wife, and

again she had agreed. And soon, the lady had a name. Her husband no longer referred to her as the lady helping him with his
papers, he now called her Rhonda. The first day she had heard
the name Rhonda she had rolled the name around in her head.
It sounded short, crisp, and authoritative. Little by little things
began to change. He needed to run a few errands for Rhonda.
He needed to take Rhonda to the movies, he needed to pay a few
of Rhonda's bills. *Oh, Rhonda has been so nice to us, I think
I need to buy her a gift.* Not long after that, he would mistak-
enly refer to Ebone as Rhonda and quickly correct himself and
look at her, his large brown eyes pleading for understanding and
asking her to trust him.

One day Rhonda called. Her husband was at work.

"This is Rhonda, I guess you know who I am," the voice at
the other end said.

"Well, yes, I know you a bit . . . ," she had responded,
mystified.

"So when are you getting your lazy ass out of the house to go
find a job so my man can move in with me?"

"Did I hear you say, 'your man'?"

"Yup, you heard right, my man, or is that in doubt?"

"I think you should call back when my husband is here, he's
in a better position to talk to you."

"There is nothing he has not told me, there is nothing more
to discuss, just get your lazy ass out of the house and go get yourself a job like a normal upright citizen, okay, remember you are
now in the good old USA, this is not Africa, okay?"

When he came in that night, she had told him about the call.
First he had feigned anger and had picked up the phone, and
then he had dropped the phone and begun to tell her to show

some understanding. She did not understand what he meant by the word *understanding*.

Then he got the eighty-thousand-dollar IT job. He had been attending classes and reading for the examinations for the past three months. He had not touched her in a long while, and claimed that it was because of the examinations. She would never know why he had gone ahead and told Rhonda that he had been offered a job, and had even told her the salary that came with the new job. "Now you are married to me for real, African man," Rhonda had screamed.

She was sure she smelled Rhonda on her husband when he came in that night. She wished they were living in the village back in Africa. She was sure the village dogs would have given him away. It was her mother who had told her the legend of the hunting dogs. The men would go hunting with the dogs, and on days that there was a kill, the dogs got something to eat. On days when the men caught nothing, the dogs went to bed hungry. The women of the village felt that this was an unfair way to treat the dogs. They were the ones who began to gather the leftovers for the dogs after the evening meal. They would call the dogs and feed them. As a way of showing appreciation for the kindness of the village women, the dogs began to tell on the men. Dogs have a keen sense of smell and can smell semen on a man many miles off. Whenever any of the men walked back from the home of a concubine, the dogs would start barking and sniffing the men's crotches. That way the wife would know what the man had been up to and scold the man accordingly. Ebone wished that she had a loyal dog in America that could sniff her husband's crotch and confirm for her that he had slept with Rhonda.

Now he was asking her to return to Nigeria. He promised to

send for her after a couple of years; by then he would have gotten his American citizenship, and she could join him as his fiancée and he would marry her all over again.

As she watched the daytime talk shows, she wished she could take her problems to Oprah or Dr. Phil. The guests on the shows talked about problems that sounded like trifles, so insignificant and minuscule compared to hers. She wondered if they would understand. Americans did not overly concern themselves with the tortuous paths immigrants took to obtain a green card and citizenship.

She had confided to another Nigerian woman, the woman who owned the African store in Silver Spring. The woman had laughed out loud and told her that the day she left America would be the last time she saw her husband.

"Suppose I leave and you never send for me ever again, what would I do?" she had asked her husband.

"And if I chose to move in with Rhonda now and never return to this house, what would you do? How would you pay the rent? In a matter of weeks you'd be thrown out of the apartment, and Immigration would bundle you back to Nigeria," her husband had responded.

She had watched the callous unfeeling words spill out of his mouth as if he had rehearsed them. He said the words without pity, looking at her straight in the eyes. And then his voice had dropped, and he had pleaded with her to trust him.

Every night she waited to hear the sound of his key turning in the lock. Was he coming back, or had he decided to move in with Rhonda? Only the click of the lock held the answer.

. . . .

Malobi's husband wanted a child. His family also wanted her to have a child, because her husband was an only child. They did not want the family name to disappear. Back in Nigeria, they pointed out decrepit houses that had been owned by rich people who had no progeny to inherit the properties after their death. Her mother-in-law sent her by courier all the way from Nigeria medicinal concoctions in dark bottles that stank horribly. How she managed to convince the courier company to ship the stuff, Malobi could never tell. One of the concoctions stank even more horribly than the previous ones. Her mother-in-law confessed to her that the base was from the urine of a female cow, and asked her if she had ever heard of a barren cow, to which she responded no. "Aha!" her mother-in-law had exclaimed, "I've been assured by the *babalawo* who prepared the medicine for me that just as there is no barren cow, you too will not be childless." The conversation had left Malobi feeling like the proverbial cow without a tail, which was said to be at the mercy of all manner of flies.

Then her husband began traveling to Nigeria every summer. He had vaguely told her that he had a project in Nigeria. The nature of the project was never fully explained. At first she assumed he was building a house, but he had told her it was not that kind of project. The military had just handed over power to a civilian government, and she thought he was perhaps pursuing a government contract. She hinted at this, but he was not forthcoming, so she let it be.

He was away on one of his trips to Nigeria when she got a call from her mother-in-law.

"Your husband is dead. Yes, he died in a car accident on the road to Abuja."

Malobi gasped and clutched tightly at the phone, her mouth

suddenly without saliva, her palm clammy, and her breath becoming faster.

"What happened? How could he be dead, I spoke with him only two days ago. . . ."

"Your husband is dead. He is my son, and I am confirming it to you."

Malobi paused and tried to read her mother-in-law's tone. There was something in that voice, some inflection she was missing, and days later, after the conversation, it came to her with the clarity of dawn. Not once had her mother-in-law said, "My son is dead"; she had kept saying "your husband."

"I am going to try and get on a flight back to Nigeria tomorrow."

"There is no need to trouble yourself with coming home. We have already buried him."

"Buried him? How can you bury my own husband in my absence?"

"He's been buried, he is dead, is all I can tell you. You have your own life to live. You are still young. There are many men in America, I am sure you will find a good man," her mother-in-law said, and the line went dead.

Malobi called the president of the Nigerian Union in Philadelphia, a balding old man with bulgy froglike eyes and a kind face, known as "Baba" by members of the Nigerian community. Though he had lived in the United States for many decades, Baba still spoke English with a very thick Nigerian accent.

Baba had laughed out loud, tears streaming out of his froglike eyes, when Malobi told him of the call from her mother-in-law.

"It is the way of our people; she means that the marriage is over," he told her. "She means her son is no longer your husband. It is the way of riddles, the way the elders spoke to each other. When the man of the house dies, they say the big tree has fallen, the thumb has been cut off, we can no longer snap the fingers. I still have contacts back home; I will make a few calls and get back to you."

He indeed made the calls, and confirmed that her husband was still alive. A few months later Baba brought her a copy of one of Nigeria's soft-sell magazines. There was a picture of her husband and his new bride beaming into the camera at the christening ceremony of their new baby at Christ's Church Cathedral.

THESE ARE OUR stories, and the stories of the men we married. Once we had dreams of growing old together and reminiscing of our early days in this land of big dreams; how could we have known that the underbelly of the black snake is white, and that the land of big dreams is also the land of huge nightmares? It is a good thing that we share our stories with the world, because we also have daughters and sisters, and they will hear these tales, our stories, and say to themselves, This will not be our fate; we will never become married widows in our own lifetime.

Nigerians in America

I was thirteen when Uncle Siloko came to live with us in Belts-ville, Maryland. Siloko was the nickname he and my father called each other, both of them having attended Siloko Grammar School back in Nigeria. He had a one-semester lectureship position in the English department at the state university. His family was in Minnesota, where he had done his graduate studies. His plan was to leave his family, a wife and a daughter, in Minnesota because he could not yet afford to rent a place. He would send for them as soon as he was settled in.

I went with my father to pick him up from the Greyhound station. He wore a well-cut black winter coat and a two-tone brown-and-black beanie. He was carrying a small bulging suit-case and another large blue bag that had "Safari" written on its four sides.

"How was the trip?" my father asked him.

"Tortuous," he responded, and laughed, a big booming laughter that made a few people at the bus station turn around and stare at us. As he laughed, he took off his beanie, folded it and put it in one of the pockets of his coat, and brought out a pack of chewing gum. He unwrapped a piece, put it in his mouth, and was about to start chewing it when he turned to my father and asked, "Why have I not had the honor of meeting the beautiful young lady?"

"My daughter, Adesua," my father said.

He looked at me and smiled and chewed vigorously on his gum. It was my first experience of meeting a grown Nigerian man who chewed gum. He smiled, and I could see the deep dimples on both sides of his face.

I curtsied and said, "Welcome, Uncle." I had been taught by my parents to address every older Nigerian male as "Uncle," and older females as "Auntie."

"Adesua, the pleasure is all mine," he said, and his laughter boomed once again. He offered me a piece of gum. I took it and threw it into my mouth and was pleasantly shocked by its strong strawberry flavor.

As we drove off in Father's car with the heat turned on full blast as usual, he began to wind down the glass on his side of the car.

"Are you hot?" my father asked.

"Oh, yes, quite hot, or have you forgotten I'm coming from Minnesota, where the major economic commodity is snow?"

He spoke like a character in a play. He had a way of making everything he said interesting. He would sometimes say something very serious and laugh, and when he was joking, he wore a very serious expression. For the entire time that he lived with us, I could never tell when he was joking and when he was serious.

I had heard my parents say that Uncle Siloko would be staying in the basement; for some reason, by the time we got home, my father had changed his mind. He moved into the room upstairs, the room next to mine and opposite my parents' bedroom. He did not stop my father from carrying his bags upstairs for him. He no doubt expected people to do things for him.

He went into the bathroom, which until that morning had been mine, to take a shower and was soon whistling in the bath. He came out smelling strongly of aftershave and was still whistling as he walked into his room. When I walked past my old bathroom, I could see through the half-open door that he had swept my cream and other stuff to one side, and his bottles and lotions now occupied half of the space before the bathroom mirror. There appeared to be such a wide array of stuff, three kinds of face cream, an aftershave lotion, aftershave balm, and other tubes and bottles.

I was downstairs watching television when he came down. My father was in the kitchen, bringing out different soups and stews from the fridge, and a half pot of water for *fufu* was boiling on the stove.

"Siloko, what will it be for you? Wetin you wan chop?" my father asked him.

"Rice, *eba*, anything—I don't care, the point is to fill the stomach," he replied.

He turned to me and began to ask me about the program I was watching on cable. He was familiar with the program and told me the name of his favorite character. He laughed at the Trix yogurt commercial and completed the slogan—"Silly rabbit, Trix are for kids."

My father called to tell us that dinner was served, and we moved to the dining table. Uncle Siloko asked for a fork and a knife to eat his *fufu*. Our visiting relatives often used their fingers to eat *fufu*. He fell on the food with gusto. He licked his lips and remarked that the soup tasted so good. He asked my father if he was the one who had made the soup, or my mother. Dad said that he was the one who cooked most of the time. He said that Mom was still at work; she was a licensed practical nurse and would be coming back late.

"You know, even when you were in boarding school, you were a remarkable cook. I remember the magic you performed with a tin of Geisha canned mackerel and a pack of Uncle Ben's rice," he said to my father. He picked his teeth and covered his mouth as he burped.

"And you, Siloko, what were you? Were you not the expert writer of love letters? Or have you forgotten how we used to bribe you with a tin of condensed milk to help us compose those special lines that never failed with the girls?"

"Ah, don't even go there," Uncle Siloko said. "I wrote the letters, but you guys got the girls."

Dad closed his eyes and began to recite in a voice that seemed to be from the past: "I write to ask if you are swimming perfectly in the ocean of good health, if so doxology. The lungs in my body flapped with joy when my orbs rested on your beautiful form. My heart is perambulating, and time and ability and double capacity has forced my pen to dance automatically on this benedicted sheet of paper. Please do not say no so my medulla oblongata does not stop functioning, until we meet, accept this blue blood on paper as a sign of my unquenchable love."

"So you still remember that after all these years?" Uncle Siloko asked my father. My father's eyes twinkled, and they appeared to be glowing. Uncle Siloko went upstairs and came down with a bottle of red wine.

"There is beer in the fridge; why did you bother to buy a bottle of wine?" my father asked.

"American beer does not fill the mouth like our Nigerian brands Gulder and Star; besides, red wine is better for the heart, or have you forgotten we are not getting any younger?" They both laughed and began to drink. Dad turned to me and asked if it was not my bedtime, but Uncle Siloko told him to let me stay around, and added that the best way for me to acquire Nigerian wisdom was by sitting at the feet of elders.

I heard the lock turn downstairs; it was Mom, returning from her job. She soon came upstairs. As she walked in, her eyes turned to where I was sitting.

"Oh, you are still awake," she said, looking up at the clock. I was about to respond when she looked toward the dining table and saw Dad with Uncle Siloko. She smiled and stretched out her hand, but Uncle Siloko brushed the proffered hand away and gently embraced her.

"Ah, you are the powerful Nigerian woman that has succeeded in taming my rascally friend?" he asked, laughing loudly.

"To God be the glory," Mom said, using one of her stock phrases that sounded like words out of a hymnal.

"Ah, who said I have been tamed?" Dad said mockingly, puffing out his chest.

"None is so hopelessly tamed as he who thinks he's not been tamed," Uncle Siloko said, and laughed.

"Do not mind my husband, *jare*," Mom said with the kind of jollity I had never heard in her voice.

"Come have a glass of wine, I'm sure you've had a tiring day," Uncle Siloko said to Mom.

"Ah, my wife hardly ever touches alcohol," Dad said.

"*Haba*, you chauvinistic Nigerian man, have you forgotten this is America? Let the woman speak for herself."

"Well, it is not that I hate alcohol, it is the smell that I dislike. You know I grew up with my grandmother in Sapele, and she used to sell *ogogoro*, what the colonialists called illicit gin. She stored it in big blue rubber jerry cans behind the door of her room. One day I went into the room, opened the gallon, and took a little sip. It burned my throat a bit but tasted so good, so I took another sip and then a large gulp. I did not know when I passed out. My grandmother came into the room and with one look noticed what had happened and forced a large quantity of palm oil down my throat. I threw up, but did not wake up until the next day. Since that day, I've never really liked the smell of alcohol, but that has not stopped your friend here from drinking his beer."

"Well, once bitten, twice shy," Uncle Siloko said in a sober tone, but then quickly added, "If you try and you do not succeed, try, try again." This time the three of them laughed together.

Turning toward me, Dad said, "You have picked up enough wisdom for one night—you had better go to your bed." Mother looked up at me in mock horror and rolled her eyes, appearing surprised that I was still awake. I left them and walked to my room. As I brushed my teeth, I could still hear their laughter from the sitting room.

That weekend, my father's friends and relatives came from Dorchester, Upper Marlboro, and as far as Virginia. I was told to call all of them "Uncle" as a way of showing respect, even though I could not say exactly how they were related to me. Uncle John Oba, the most jovial of the lot, who would usually introduce himself by saying, "My name is John Oba or Oba John, whichever you prefer," was the first to arrive. He came in carrying two cartons of Guinness Draught. I knelt down in greeting before him, but he looked unhappy and had no jokes for me today.

"Oba John or John Oba, which should I call you today?" Dad called out to him, smiling and stretching out his hands.

"I don't know, Uncle; I don't know who I am anymore. That foolish African American girl Sheniqua wants to ruin my life."

"Our lives are in God's hands; no human has the power to destroy them," Dad responded.

"She called up the INS and told them that the marriage I contracted with her was fake. She told them that I paid her for the purposes of getting a green card."

Uncle Siloko, who was taking a nap upstairs, soon walked into the sitting room. He had showered and shaved and was wearing a blue cotton dashiki. Father introduced him to John Oba as his friend the professor. Uncle Siloko objected to being called a professor; he said he was only a visiting lecturer. That still makes you a professor, John Oba said, and shook his hand while bowing slightly.

Soon the others arrived, Uncle Sunny and Uncle Ikpanwosa, who had shortened his name to Ik. The conversation turned once again to Uncle John's problem.

"What really happened, or should I say, how exactly did this happen?" Dad asked him.

"I did not know that the *yeye* girl had opened over four credit card accounts in my name. She has all my information, including my social—you know my mail goes to her house, a few of my clothes and shoes are there too, you can never tell when the INS will visit just to be sure we are living together. When they sent the applications for the cards to her address, she filled them out and blew the money, she maxed out all the cards, and I did not even know about this. It was only when I tried to open a charge account with Sears and my application was denied that I sensed something was wrong. I sent off for my credit report that same week and discovered what she had done. I was very angry and rushed to her house and confronted her. I called her names. At first she seemed contrite; then she got angry and swore she was going to send my sorry ass back to Africa. This is the same girl who I've been paying four hundred dollars every two weeks."

"I think you overreacted. You know what we say in Nigeria— when you want to kill a tsetse fly perched on your scrotum, you approach the task gingerly," Dad said.

"Do you mind if I say something?" Uncle Siloko asked.

"*Haba!* Siloko, you do not need anyone's permission to say something, or aren't you one of us anymore?" Dad said.

"Money is at the root of this problem, and money can be used to resolve it too. Just call her, apologize, and offer her more money—tell her you are increasing her biweekly payment by an extra hundred dollars, and you'll see what happens."

"But she's already called the INS, and they've written to me to appear before them within ninety days."

"Have you forgotten what we say in Nigeria, that the same people who invented the pencil also invented the eraser? Just the same way she called them, she could still call them back and tell them that she lied, that she was only angry with you. You can even convince her that she should go with you to their office."

This seemed to cheer Uncle John and every other person up. Drinks were opened, the music of Dombraye Aghama was slotted into the tape player. Uncle Sunny soon changed the topic to Nigeria.

"So, Professor, do you think these soldiers—I mean the khaki boys that are ruling the country—do you think they'll ever hand it over to politicians?"

"When soldiers overrun any place, they rape and loot, and that is what they are doing to Nigeria. They are raping and stealing the country blind, along with their civilian supporters. If not for them, what would I be doing in this cold country?" he asked.

"But it was the civilians that invited the military to overthrow the democratically elected government. I don't think we are ripe for democracy," Uncle Ikpanwosa added.

"No country is ever ripe for democracy. Democracy has to grow and ripen wherever it finds a fertile ground. Even here in this country, it is because the people worked for it—that is why they have a democracy."

Uncle Sunny asked about Uncle Siloko's family and how soon they'd be coming to join him in Maryland.

"As soon as I get my first salary and settle in a bit, I will get a place and move them over here," he said.

Everyone talked about how cold Minnesota was and swore that they could never live there. This seemed true to me, because even though the heater in our house was set to the high eighties, they all still wore their coats indoors and folded their arms around their chests.

Dad, who had all the while been in the kitchen preparing *fufu*, invited all of them down to the dining table. The visitors began to eat; it was only Uncle Siloko who asked if I was not going to join them.

"*Haba*, how can she sit with men like us to eat? If not for the fact that we are in America, would she be sitting here with us?

She would be with the womenfolk in the kitchen, adding more firewood to the fire," my dad said, and all the men laughed.

Uncle Sunny, who worked in the state correctional facility, commented that there was an increase in the number of inmates in the state prison who had Nigerian names. He said that they were mostly young people born here in America to Nigerian parents. He complained that most of them did not even speak any Nigerian language.

"And do you know they are all inside for drug-related offenses?"

"It has to be drugs or credit card fraud," Dad said. "Did you not hear the story of the old white lady in D.C. whose house was burgled, and she called the cops and told them she suspected that some Nigerian boys who lived in the opposite apartment must be responsible. The cops laughed and told her that Nigerians do not dirty their hands with petty burglary—'When Nigerians steal, they steal big,' the cops said and left." Everyone laughed, and then there was silence. The visitors soon left.

Later that night I heard Uncle Siloko speaking with his wife on the phone. He was telling her how he could not wait for her and his daughter to join him. He said that Maryland was just like Nigeria, and not isolated like Minnesota. They spoke for a very long time, and sometimes his voice dropped to a low whisper.

Things appeared not to be going well for Uncle Siloko in his new job. He complained to Dad about his students. They came to class with a hangover and hardly made comments or responded to his questions. The worst part was that he had been assigned a female professor, Ava Wilson, as some kind of mentor but more of a supervisor. She was to visit his class and watch his teaching, and she would look at his graded papers. He said that to make matters worse, he had found out that after insurance deductions, his take-home pay was going to be quite small, and not enough to take him home. And then he added that that was not even the worst part. He was not assigned a proper office but had to share a large hall with a bunch of teaching assistants. Dad told him not to worry so much, that it was only a matter of time before things settled down a bit. I suspected Uncle Siloko was not going to be making any contributions toward the rent, and this turned out to be true.

Uncle Siloko began coming back late from the school. He refused to eat and would go straight to his room, and within a few short minutes I would hear his loud snores from upstairs, though I was sitting at the dining table downstairs doing my homework. He would not stay and talk with Dad the way he used to, and each time they talked, he always brought up the name of Professor Ava Wilson. It was tax season, and a busy time for Dad. He was the one who filed taxes for most of our Nigerian relatives and other West Africans. It was the only time of the year that he worked, and I had learned over the years not to disturb him during this period.

Even Mom, who was hardly ever home, began to notice Uncle Siloko's absences.

"I hardly see your friend these days, is his job taking all his time?"

"He's very busy at his job," Dad answered curtly and went back to looking at W-2 forms.

It was time for my social studies project, and I was at a loss for a topic to work on. It was not a good time to talk with Dad about this. I do not remember how Uncle Siloko heard about my assignment, but he offered to help and fell into the project with lots of enthusiasm. He proposed that I title my project "Ni-gerians in America." I would talk about the culture of Nigeri-ans in America. I would talk about their foods, music, dances, language, clothes, and all the things that had followed them from Nigeria and how they were still stuck with these things. He suggested that I wear some beads on my hair on the day of my presentation, and play some Nigerian music. My project presentation went very well, and Mr. Lobb, my teacher, gave me extra credit for being detailed. I was grateful to Uncle Siloko but didn't have a chance to thank him because he was hardly ever at home.

I heard my parents talking about Uncle Siloko.

"And I thought he was a godly man. What about his wife and his daughter? He does not even talk about bringing them over anymore. Now he wants to bring a white woman to my house, Ava Wilson, or is it Abba Wilson he calls her?"

"America changes people. He is a grown man, and free to make his choices," my father said.

"You are not even thinking about your daughter," my mom said, gesturing toward my room, obviously unaware that I was listening to their conversation.

"What about my daughter? What has this got to do with her?" my dad asked.

"Oh, you mean you don't know she's almost a woman now, you want her to think it's okay for married people to have af-fairs, eh? Does the Abba, or is it Ava, woman know that your friend is even married?" Mom asked.

"It wouldn't surprise me if she knows—some of them don't care. After all, she is not Nigerian," my dad said.

"In that case, I owe it to his wife to let her know," Mom said.

"Hmmm," Dad responded, sighing.

"And all the money he's been spending going to D.C. bars with her, can he not at least contribute something to this house?"

"I already told you, I do not want him to contribute anything," Dad responded.

"A white woman in this house, oh, wonders shall never end," Mom said.

"What is wrong is wrong, it does not matter if she's black or white," Dad said.

Mom had always vaguely discouraged me from making white friends. Even when I was much younger and my third-grade teacher, Mrs. Pomeroy, had made a telephone directory of all of us in her class and had encouraged us to call each other on weekends, Mom had objected. I recall her saying that it was not that white people were not good, it was just that we were not the same. When a classmate of mine, Mariah Schroder, had called the house, inviting me for a sleepover, Mom had lied to her that I was not home, that I had gone to spend the weekend at my uncle's place in Largo. Later that week, Mariah had asked me if I had fun at Largo; for a moment I had forgotten my mother's lie and hesitated, and then I had told her Largo was fun. Later Mom had tried to explain to me why my friends could not sleep over. Our Nigerian food would be too spicy for them; they would come back to school with tales of the things we ate and the way we lived. I believed her.

All through that week, Uncle Siloko came home very late. I heard him telling Dad that he was grading papers. He would come in and go straight to the bathroom. He would then head to his room and would start snoring not long thereafter. Long gone were the days of talking with Dad past midnight.

Ava Wilson's visit started off on a wrong note. When she pulled into our driveway with Uncle Siloko, we all looked out through the window blinds. She stepped out of the car, a smallish woman with dyed red hair. She shut the door of the car, and as Uncle Siloko stepped out, she whispered something to him. They both looked up, and then she put her hand in her bag and brought out a pack of cigarettes. She lit up and blew up the smoke furiously. It was a cold day, and she was wearing a big winter coat that looked like a man's and almost swallowed her up.

"Oh, so she smokes?" my mom said, and hissed and walked to the kitchen.

When they both came inside, Dad welcomed her, smiling and fussing over her, but Mom greeted her with a tight smile and walked back to the kitchen. Ava asked for coffee, but coffee was hardly drunk in our house, though Mom managed to find a sachet of instant decaf somewhere in one of the kitchen cupboards.

Mom served the meal of rice and stew and vegetable salad that she had been busy preparing in the kitchen. Ava, who had earlier said she loved spicy food, tasted the rice and stew, and her face turned red; instantly she asked for water, and after taking a few sips sat staring at the food. She never went back to it, but finished her coffee.

"My friend, well, not my friend, my brother has told me how helpful you have been to him in the school, thank you so much," my dad said.

"He exaggerates," Ava said, smiling and looking at Uncle Siloko, who had been surprisingly quiet.

"When his wife and daughter join him here, we will all come and say thank you properly," Mom chimed in.

"What's that?" Ava asked. The way she said it made both words run together.

"My wife is saying that when my friend's wife here joins him from Minnesota, we will all get together for dinner with you to show our appreciation," my Dad said, smiling.

Uncle Siloko stood up, and Ava stood up too. She said she had to be going, since she did not like to drive at night. When they both left, Mom looked at Dad and Dad looked at her, and they both clasped each other's right hand like wrestlers in a ring and began to laugh.

By the time Uncle Siloko came back that night, I was already in bed. A few days later he moved out. He told dad that he had found a place in College Park; it was close to campus, and he would be sharing the place with a Ugandan grad student.

We later heard that his contract was not renewed at the college, and he went back to Minnesota at the beginning of spring. The last time Dad heard about him, he had returned to Nigeria to run for the chairmanship position in his state's local government elections.

I Will Lend You My Wife

Nduka sounded very excited on the phone when he called. She could hear him panting like a heavy smoker who had been forced to do a hundred-meter dash.

"I have paid someone to bring you in. He will invite you to America as his fiancée. He is African American. He will send you a letter that you'll take to the embassy. They respect their own people. I am sure they will honor the letter. I paid him well; I paid him thirty-five hundred dollars." The words rushed out of his mouth. He did not wait to hear her questions, but went right on tabulating his plans.

"Baby, you see I have not been sleeping, I have been working hard for you to join me over here. Greet Papa and Mama—I will speak with them when next I call, okay?"

Ijedi was happy; finally she was leaving for America to join her husband. There was hardly anything she had not tried to get a visa after Nduka left for the United States. On one occasion she had gone to a pastor to bless her international passport before she went for her visa interview at the embassy. She re-membered the pastor's words.

"As soon as they open your passport, they will be blinded by the anointing." He sprinkled olive oil on the pages of the pass-port; he turned to her and stared into her eyes.

"As soon as they are blinded by the anointing, they will have no choice but to honor your request; they will be so over-whelmed by the fire that they will do your bidding." And the pastor laughed in a maniacal manner like a hyena, grabbed her head with his two hands, and began to spit out incantations in a strange language at her.

She had left with her heavily stained passport after leaving some money in a white envelope for the pastor. She recalled that the interview at the embassy had lasted only a few minutes. The consular officer, a sunburned American lady who looked like a retired school headmistress, turned to Ijedi as she flipped through the passport, taking in the olive-oil-stained pages.

"Why should I issue you a United States visa when I have no guarantees that you are going to return to your country after your visit, as you claim? I don't see any ties binding you to your country."

"I have a large shop where I sell provisions and clothes," Ijedi said. She was scared; the woman's eyes were green, the exact color of her grandmother's cat that had returned to the wild after living with them for several years.

"I am not convinced there is enough incentive for you to return; how much do you make each year from your provisions store?" Cat Eyes asked.

"About two million naira," Ijedi lied bravely, even as the lie attempted to stick in her throat. She managed to scrape only a couple of thousands of naira as profit after all the taxes and levies she had to pay to the state and local government.

"Do you have any children?" the woman asked.

"No, none yet."

"Any houses, landed property, things of value like stocks, bonds, shares, trust funds, and annuities?" she asked, again the words rolling off her tongue in mockery.

"No, I do not have any of the things you mentioned."

The woman pulled out a heavy stamp and stamped furiously on Ijedi's anointed passport, some of the ink splashing on the white sheets of paper on her table.

Ijedi walked out of the embassy like a rain-soaked vulture, her mind reeling, restraining herself from calling Nduka right away. He would just be waking up at that hour, since Nigerian time was six hours ahead. She hissed at nobody in particular and waved down a passing yellow cab.

A YEAR AFTER their wedding, Nduka had lost his job at the bank. It was a small but very well-managed bank that had been bought by a bigger bank in the restructuring of the banking sector. The bank had been kind enough to give him a generous severance package. When Nduka showed her the letter of retrenchment, she had broken down in tears.

"It is my fault, everyone is going to blame me for bringing bad luck into your life, people will say I'm a bad-luck woman, that you were doing well before you married me, and now you have lost your job."

"Why are you so concerned about what people are going to say? I think you should be more worried about us, about our survival, about our future, about the children we are going to have . . . ," Nduka said, trailing off.

"But you know how it is. Your parents have been worried that I am not yet pregnant, and now to have this on top of that is just too much for me. What am I going to do?"

Nduka had stormed out at that point. She knew he was going to the drinking place down the road to meet with his friend Emeka, whom everyone referred to as his "second wife." Emeka was his childhood friend and had been the best man at their wedding. He was still a bachelor, even though he was doing well and ran his own advertising agency. Every night, after taking his dinner, Nduka would join Emeka in the beer parlor down the road, and they would drink and smoke till after midnight. In the early days of their marriage, Ijedi had followed Nduka to the place and had sat down with them while sipping a malt drink. She had been disappointed by everything. They just sat there, occasionally exchanging some dry jokes in code and calling for more beer and cigarettes. Ijedi was surprised there were no girls in the place. Someone had told her that single girls went to some of the drinking places to hook up with men who were drunk and therefore generous.

Nduka came back from the bar in high spirits. He said Emeka had promised to help him get an American visa. He would give him a letter to the embassy, stating that Nduka was one of Emeka's senior executives who was going for an advertising workshop in America. The ruse had worked, and Nduka had been issued a visa. Since he left, he had been sending money to Ijedi for her to join him, but she had found it impossible to get a visa.

People had told her she was lucky that Nduka had not

forgotten her. She had her in-laws to thank for that. They had been behind her, writing letters to their son and making expensive international telephone calls to America.

She got a fresh passport and went to the embassy with the documents and pictures that Nduka sent. She had a fairly easy time. She concluded that it must be because everyone loved a love story.

"How did you get to meet your fiancé?" the consular officer asked her.

"He saw my picture with my cousin who lives in the United States, he told him he liked me, he got my e-mail address and telephone number from my cousin, and we have been communicating ever since."

"And you say you have never met; how can you marry a man you have never met? I mean, it is kind of strange."

"My father married my mother through a photograph his family sent to him; they never met until their wedding day, and they are still happily married," Ijedi responded.

This seemed to break the ice, and the consular officer listened to Ijedi's narrative about how her father had been sent a photograph of her schoolteacher mother by his parents, and he had told them to go ahead and marry the bride for him. Ijedi was given the visa. It was called a K-1 visa and was for people who were joining their American fiancés. The visa rules stipulated that the couple must get married within ninety days. Nduka had told her that she would live with her "husband" for some time, for appearance's sake. Besides, the immigration officers had been known to visit to confirm that husband and wife were actually living together.

. . . .

Nduka came to meet her at the airport with her "husband."
His name was Jonathan Smokes; he was tall and gangly and reminded her vaguely of a character from the television comedy
Good Times. He wore his hair in curls and spoke in a soft sing-
song voice that she would grow to love in the days to come.

Nduka gave her a big hug. He hadn't changed much. He just
looked a lot less relaxed than he used to be, and a bit impatient.
She did not blame him. She had already noticed that the pace of
life was faster here than what she was used to back in Nigeria.
People spoke faster; she had to strain her ears to hear the questions the immigration officer asked her. The immigration officer
had made a joke about mind over matter that she did not get but
laughed about.

"We will sleep at Jonathan's place," Nduka told her. When
she asked him why he had told her to be patient, he responded,
"This is America."

Jonathan's apartment was tiny but very clean and beautiful.
The walls were painted white, which added a touch of cleanli-
ness to the place. Pictures of chubby-cheeked children—he said
they were his nieces and nephews—adorned the walls. It also
began to dawn on her that it was no coincidence that the guy's
last name was Smokes. He smoked a lot of cigarettes; otherwise
he was very nice, called her I-Jay, and smiled a lot.

Ijedi was surprised that he had put on an apron and gone to
the kitchen to cook for them. After having a bath they had joined
him in the kitchen. Nduka had whispered to her that Jonathan
was a marvelous cook. She asked to help him out, but he only
smiled and told her he was fine. In a corner of the kitchen was

a hair dryer and piles of *Ebony* and *Essence* magazines. Nduka said Jonathan was a hairdresser, and Jonathan smiled at her, touching her hair and commenting on its fine texture. Ijedi was surprised that Nduka only smiled when Jonathan touched her hair. The old Nduka would not have let anyone touch his woman.

She enjoyed the meal prepared by Jonathan. There was a bit of everything. It was as if they were eating out, and to top it off he made each of them a cup of coffee. And he did all of this smiling and seemed to be enjoying every minute of it. He even gave his bedroom to them.

That night she was happy to be in Nduka's arms again; they enjoyed each other. Their lovemaking before he left Nigeria had been beginning to lose the tenderness of their early days because of the pressure of her not yet getting pregnant. They had discovered each other again, and she felt happy.

Nduka explained to her why he could not take her home. He had no home; he worked for a haulage company and lived out of a truck. He told her that was how he had managed to save up money to send for her. He said Jonathan was a very good friend who had agreed to assist them. He told her he was leaving the next morning for Delaware and would not be back till after a week. She wanted to ask him if he was not worried about leaving her alone with Jonathan but thought better of it, since it also meant she was bringing into question her own faithfulness. She followed him to the truck. It was quite nice, and the inside was cozy too. She could now see how he could live comfortably in the truck for weeks.

By the time she took a nap and woke up, Jonathan had cleaned the entire house. The floor, which was made of wooden boards, was gleaming, and everywhere smelled of Pine-Sol. He was wearing an apron again and was in the kitchen expertly peeling the skin off a piece of fresh chicken, cutting it in cubes, rolling it in chili spice, and putting it into an oven tray.

"Nd told me you like spicy food, so I'm making you something really hot and spicy," he said.

"Oh, no, you should have let me do the cooking this time; in my country men do not cook."

"Oh, really? Men don't cook—that's weird," he said and began to laugh.

"But it is true, cooking is seen as a woman's job. Even sweeping the house; I was shocked to see you doing that."

"Wow, that must really be hard for the women. You mean Nd never helped you out in the kitchen when you guys were in Nigeria? That must have really been hard; he told me you had your own business establishment. So how did you juggle that?"

"It was not that difficult. In my country women juggle a whole lot more, including large families and full-time jobs. It is even worse in the rural areas, where the women do all the work and the men sit under the trees drinking *ogogoro*, local gin."

Before they went to sleep that night, Jonathan sat across from her in his pink pajamas and slowly began to roll a small marijuana cigarette. Smiling, he offered it to her after he took the first drag. She told him she did not smoke, but that she had an uncle back home in Nigeria who did.

"My uncle thinks that the only way to achieve world peace is through ganja."

"Oh, really? Tell me 'bout this uncle of yours. I'm beginning to like him already."

"He was an ex-soldier. He fought in the Biafran war and

came back from the war with a limp and seven bullets lodged in his thigh. He had nothing after the war and started a marijuana farm. He came back home with all kinds of animals every day from his farm; he said the animals became jolly and dozed off after eating the marijuana leaves and seeds. He picked them up with his hands and used them to prepare delicious stews. My mother warned me not to eat the stew. She claimed he added ganja leaves to it, but I always ate it secretly, and often left his house feeling happy."

"Oh, my! You must have eaten the marijuana without knowing it."

"No, I doubt it. My uncle would not have done anything to endanger my well-being."

"Who told you marijuana would interfere with your well-being?" Jonathan said, laughing.

He smoked the marijuana until it was completely gone and had to put the tips of his fingers to his tongue because he had burned them slightly. She went to him and took his hands, took him to the washbasin in the bathroom, and poured cold water on them. She could smell the almost raw smell of the ganja on his breath and his body, but surprisingly, she liked it. She held on to his fingers after turning up the tap, and then let go of them quickly, catching herself. He only smiled and went to the fridge and poured a drink of apple juice for them both. She took a seat in the sitting room and sipped her drink slowly, crushing the ice with her teeth and enjoying it as she used to when she was small.

He began to talk to her. He told her about his grandfather, the Reverend Smokes, who always dreamed of returning to Africa. He said he wanted to be buried in the land of his ancestors. Unfortunately ill health had made him so poor that by the time he became old, there was no money to fly him to Africa. He had died an unhappy man. He told her some of his relations in Memphis said they had seen his ghost on occasion in the fog of the Delta mist. She enjoyed the story, but she was yawning. He took her hand, kissed her on the cheeks, and led her to the bed. He tucked her into bed and turned on the night lamp, gently closed the door, and went to the living room to sleep.

They went to city hall and had the wedding. Nduka was there, and they all laughed through the entire ceremony, making the officiating person remark that he had not seen such a happy couple in a very long while.

Later that night she asked Nduka why he had felt confident enough to leave her with Jonathan. She told him that she was happy he was very confident about her, even after a year of separation. Nduka only smiled, told her that he could trust Jonathan completely, and remarked mysteriously, "This is America." She began running her fingers over his hairy chest. In the sitting room, Jonathan lit a stick of marijuana.

Miracle Baby

Every summer Ijeoma's mother-in-law asked her to come to Nigeria to seek a solution to her childlessness. The previous year she had sent Ijeoma a video recording of Nigeria's latest miracle pastor. The pastor's name was Jehoshaphat. He had a long, well-groomed beard. He was shown in the video sending women into brief trances by gently blowing air onto their faces. He was said to visit barren women in their dreams and hand them babies wrapped in a white shawl. After the dream visitation, the women usually became pregnant and came to his church with their newborn babies wrapped in white shawls. The videocassette was filled with images of women singing and dancing their way to the microphone and telling stories of how Pastor Jehoshaphat had visited them in their dreams, and a few days later they had become pregnant. Some of the women told stories of how they had gone to a witch doctor, a *babalawo*, in search of a solution to their childlessness and had been made to do all kinds of weird things. A woman in the tape said that she had been made to drink cow urine for nine months, "No water, only cow urine from a white cow, for nine months." She emphasized each word. And yet she could not become pregnant. Another woman gleefully confessed that a *babalawo* had told her that the only way she could get pregnant was if she let him have his way with her. The *babalawo* was a wrinkled, toothless ninety-year-old. She confessed that she was so desperate she had slept with the man, and yet she had remained barren. Now she was the proud mother of twins after being visited by Pastor Jehoshaphat in her dream. There was another testimony by a woman who had been driven out of her matrimonial home by an irate mother-in-law. She said her mother-in-law wouldn't let her grown-up daughters eat out of the same plate or drink from the same cup with her out of fear that she would infect them with her barrenness. She said after she got pregnant, the same mother-in-law had come to beg her forgiveness and was in fact in church with her today. The mother-in-law leaped out of her seat and walked to the microphone, and both women embraced each other. The crowd erupted, and lots of white shawls went up in the air like cotton buds in the Harmattan wind.

There was yet another video testimony by a woman who claimed to have been married to a "spirit husband." She said she had had a pact with her spirit husband; that she would come to earth, get married to a man and cause her earthly husband unhappiness, and then die during childbirth and return to her spirit husband. But she had ended up falling in love with her earthly husband due to his caring nature, and had become reluctant to return to her spirit husband. This had made the spirit husband angry, and he would come into her bed every night and make love to her furiously. As a result of this, she was always too tired to make love to her earthly husband and would sometimes wake up in the morning to find her own side of the bed soaked with sweat from the lovemaking with her spirit husband. A friend had brought her to the church, and the pastor had delivered her from the powers of the spirit husband. She became pregnant and was now the mother of twins. She got a standing ovation for her testimony.

Ijeoma lived in New York City and did in fact have access to some of the best gynecologists. But her mother-in-law told her that there was nothing wrong with looking for a "homegrown solution" to her problem. People in the Nigerian community told her she was lucky to have a mother-in-law who looked out for her. In many instances the mother-in-law would have sent her out of the marriage by bringing a nubile young girl for her son. Ijeoma had grown up living with her mother-in-law, and called her Mama. She had been sent to live with the woman who later became her mother-in-law by her parents when she was quite young, in order, in her mother's words, to "receive good home training and to become a modern lady." Her future mother-in-law was a schoolteacher and a caterer, and Ijeoma had been one of many girls sent by their parents to live with her. She had taken a special interest in Ijeoma, and by the time Ijeoma had lived with her for a few months, she announced that Ijeoma would be the wife of one of her sons. Though Ijeoma had never met the man who would become her husband, she was considered fortunate by the other girls because he was living in America. His name was Juwah, and he was said to be brilliant and kind and was his mother's favorite.

Ijeoma's mother-in-law had a favorite saying: "Ignore what's written on the body of the truck, and just get into the truck." This was her mantra. She was a devout Catholic who never missed mass and was a member of the Catholic Women's League, yet she believed in the new "miracle pastors," as they were called in Nigeria. She also believed that when it came to curing Ijeoma of her childlessness, no solution was heathen. Once Ijeoma had suggested that the problem might actually be with Juwah, but her mother-in-law would not hear of it. Childlessness was always the woman's problem, even if it was not always her fault, she had told Ijeoma. She had stopped short of telling her mother-in-law that Juwah, who was a computer programmer and worked from home, was always sitting in front of the computer, and each time he came to bed, his hands and lips were cold and his touch chilly like that of a corpse.

During an earlier visit home, Ijeoma's mother-in-law had taken her to visit the popular Baby Market in Ajangbadi, a rundown part of Lagos. As they got out of the car, a couple of girls with faces turned yellow by skin-lightening creams crowded around them.

"What type of baby do you want? Boy or girl? Or even twins—I can have them for you if you pay me very well and take care of me," one of the girls said to Ijeoma. Even that early in the day, the girl's breath reeked of *ogogoro* and cigarettes.

"Sister, I have customers from London and Germany, and I have their letters to prove it, I can help you. I have given birth to many fine babies, and there is no sickness in my body—I have my doctor's report here," another of the girls said, thrusting a sheaf of stained light brown papers into her face. All around them young men stood around smoking marijuana and smilingly watched the conversation and negotiations. There were other well-dressed women there, busy negotiating with the girls.

What had grown into the Baby Market had been going on un-
derground for years but had now come into the open because of
the downturn in the economy. For a long time, many rich barren
women would go to "white-garment churches" and come back
home months later with babies. Quite often, the pastors of the
white-garment churches had a flock of young men and women
who were in their employ. Once there was a demand for a baby,
the young people were given the go-ahead to sleep together.
As soon as the girl got pregnant and had the baby, she and the
young man were paid off and the baby handed over to the barren
woman, who paid handsomely for the baby and walked away
with it, no questions asked. There were no adoption agencies
in the country, and the idea of adoption was frowned upon. Besides, no adopted person could inherit any property at the death
of his adopted parents. The relations of the deceased would
simply throw him out, referring to him as an outsider.

Turning to her mother-in-law, Ijeoma had whispered that
they should go to one corner of the Baby Market to talk pri-
vately. Thinking they were going to talk about money, one of the
young men had accosted them and started to explain. "Auntie,"
he said to Ijeoma, "are you married to a white man? Don't worry,
we have many half-castes among us here who can give you a very
yellow baby—even, *sef*, when your white husband sees the baby,
he will swear that the baby is his own, I swear to God." Ijeoma
looked at her mother-in-law and began to drag her toward the
car, but the young man was unrelenting.

"Or is it the money that you are worried about? We accept in-
stallment payment, *sef*—even if you are living abroad in London,
America, or Rome you can go with your baby and send us our
money month by month through Western Union money transfer,

and don't worry yourself about any problem in the future, we can never come to ask for the baby, in fact we sign a guarantee paper and we even swear with Bible and *ogun* if you like that we can never come to disturb you or try to take away the baby."

Ijeoma had dragged her mother-in-law away at that point, fighting to control her rising temper.

"Mama, don't you see that most of them are drug addicts and drunks—who knows the kind of sickness they are harboring?"

"Everybody who needs a baby in Lagos comes here to patronize them, and there has never been any complaint concerning them," her mother-in-law replied.

"But Mama, for these people it is only a business, and a baby should be conceived in love. A child is not a commodity, you know."

"It is you who will give the baby love when he is born, not these people," her mother-in-law replied with her sometimes impeccable logic. But Ijeoma had not been convinced. She suggested that she needed time to think things over and promised that they could return the next week when she had thought sufficiently about it.

"My daughter, it is because I want to carry your baby on my knees before I die—this is why I am doing all of these things. Don't forget that I am getting old and I cannot be with you forever," she said to Ijeoma in a tone that sounded woebegone but wheedling.

By the time they went back to the Baby Market a week later, the place had been raided by the police. There were reports that some Lagos women were using the babies they bought from the place for moneymaking *juju* rituals. A few months later, the Baby Market resurfaced in a new location and was said to have grown even bigger. It now had the police on its payroll and was receiving police protection. All that had happened during her last visit, and this time she was hoping things would be different. She had no wish to return to the Baby Market.

The weekend after Ijeoma arrived, her mother-in-law chartered a taxi to take them to a church in Badagry, on the outskirts of Lagos, where the prophet's church was located. Badagry used to be the center of a famous slave market in the days of slavery, which housed the place that used to be known as the "point of no return." It was said that once a captured slave reached this spot, he had no chance of ever going back. It was said that to this day, the slaves' voices could still be heard, crying out that they did not want to leave their fatherland. It was now a tourist destination; there was also a Museum of Slavery that housed chains, shackles, and other paraphernalia of that infamous trade in black people.

The prophet's church was a large white hall surrounded by canopies and tents. Behind it were little shacks made out of palm fronds. Members of the church and supplicants who had traveled from afar wore white flowing gowns and walked about on bare feet; the prophet had designated the location of his church a holy ground, and no shoes were allowed. All around women and children in dirty white soutanes sat waiting. Some of the children played in the sand, while a few played in puddles of urine. There were flies everywhere, and the heat was stifling. The majority of those waiting had apparently been fasting, and their lips appeared to be coated in a white film. Big cooking pots were boiling atop large fires, and the smell of boiling beef and rice filled the air. According to a brochure that Ijeoma bought at the entrance to the church, the prophet had started out as a carpenter and coffin maker. One day while he was in the bush, cutting wood, a little black bird had called out his name. As he stood still listening to the voice of the bird, he had fallen into a deep trance, and when he woke up, a voice had spoken to him and told him that from that day onward he would become a giver of life, rather than a taker who built coffins with which people were buried.

Ijeoma and her mother-in-law were given round plastic numbered disks and sat on white plastic chairs awaiting their turn. The inside of the church smelled of burning incense, candles, and unwashed bodies.

After a while, a female usher called their number, took them in to the presence of the prophet, and commanded them to kneel. The prophet laid a moist warm palm on Ijeoma's head and began to intone in a voice that had the raspiness of an angry night masquerade.

"You have traveled far, woman; you have crossed many waters to come to me. Ah, you have many powerful enemies, and their wish is to make your life akin to that of a barren she-goat, cursed to be always wandering and never finding rest. They locked your womb with a padlock, melted the key, and threw it into the bottom of the ocean; their one wish is that your womb will never be unlocked. But you have a powerful prayer warrior in the person of your mother-in-law here. We shall find that key and unlock your womb, and you shall be a mother not just once but seven times, yes, seven times you shall be a mother."

The prophet began to twirl around and move jerkily on his feet, his face and white soutane quickly becoming damp with sweat. He began to scream in a strange language that was an admixture of French, Greek, and his native Egun language. When he stopped, he took Ijeoma by the hand and led her to a pond behind the church. The water on the pond was clear and tinged with a touch of light blue; the sight made Ijeoma feel a bit cooler. Ijeoma could see many small fish swimming in the water. Pointing at the fish in the pond, the prophet spoke to Ijeoma.

"These are all children; these are all babies waiting to be born. Look closely, and tell me the one that you like."

Ijeoma was confused for a moment; all she could see were fish swimming in the clear water. Her mother-in-law nudged her, and she bent her neck and peered closely at the fishpond. She saw a tiny white fish with a little black stripe on its side. She pointed at it. The prophet smiled.

"You have chosen very well; that is a beautiful baby girl that you have picked."

He took them back inside. Ijeoma was already beginning to feel dizzy from the sun, the heat, the smell of incense, and peering at the clear water of the pond.

"We cannot thank you enough, man of God; so what can we give you as offering?" Ijeoma's mother-in-law asked.

"Some people choose to buy me cars—I have more cars than I can count, I have even given out many to my assistants. Some people build me houses, but I can only sleep in one house at a time. An important man that I prayed for even wanted to pull down this church and promised to build a new one in its place within seven days, but I told him not to worry, for it is not the size of the building that matters but the power of the anointing. So what I am saying is that it is up to you to give whatever you want to as a love offering—yes, that is what it is, a love offering, because you cannot buy or pay for the anointing. I see that you have crossed many seas to come here, so give us whatever it is that you people eat in that part of the world that you live in," the prophet said, rubbing his sweaty palms together.

Ijeoma dipped her hand in her bag and brought out five hundred dollars in hundred-dollar bills. The prophet took it, looked at it, and smiled.

"This is very good money. I like its color and the way it smells; it has traveled far to come and meet me, and I thank you for it. I demand nothing, only that you bring your baby here when you deliver so I can anoint her with holy water and olive oil to protect her from the eyes of the wicked, that is all I ask," he said, smiling. He rang a bell, and an usher came and led them out back to their waiting taxi.

On the ride back, Ijeoma began to think of asking her mother-in-law questions about what had happened at the prophet's. She was tired and weary, and something inside her had recoiled at the prophet's reference to the little fishes in the pond as children. She knew that this was probably the last time she would be coming to Nigeria in search of a solution to her childlessness to please her mother-in-law. She loved her mother-in-law and did not want to hurt her, but had decided that she would convince Juwah to bring her over to come and live with them in New York. But she had also heard that there were Nigerian white-garment churches and *babalawo*s in parts of Brooklyn. She wondered whether her mother-in-law would go searching for them, but also realized that her mother-in-law might not be able to navigate the confusing subway system in New York City.

The traffic began to crawl; they had been caught up in a "go-slow," a typical Lagos traffic jam. All around them were vendors selling iced water in plastic bags, DVDs, videotapes, and all kinds of imported Chinese plastic toys.

A woman whose shriveled breasts were exposed, and who carried a very young baby with kohl-lined eyes, knocked on the window of the cab. She gestured with her hand to her mouth, apparently asking for money to feed herself and the baby. Ijeoma began fumbling with her purse, searching for loose change, but her mother-in-law stopped her.

"Don't give her anything—they are all tricksters. The baby is not hers. She hired the baby from the real mother. She knows that with a baby in her arms she's likely to get more sympathy and receive more alms. Whatever she gets at the end of the day, she'll share with the child's real mother."

"You mean a woman would loan out her baby to be used for begging in the hot sun?"

"Of course—they do it all the time. The real mother of the baby probably has more than ten children and not enough money to feed them. As our people say, 'A headless man often owns many caps.' "

As the traffic began to ease up, Ijeoma threw a few notes out of the window to the beggar woman, who picked up the notes, touched them to her face, and began to pray for Ijeoma. As they drove away, Ijeoma waved at the woman, and her mother-in-law hissed.

"If you give money to all the beggars on the roads of Lagos, you'll become a beggar soon yourself," she said to Ijeoma.

"I was thinking you'll come and live with us in America. Juwah will be very happy to have you live with us," Ijeoma said to her mother-in-law, trying to change the subject.

"Me live in America—God forbid. I have heard all sorts of things about the place. I don't think it is a place for people of my age. I think the cold will kill me, and besides, how can I live in a place where I hear some people will have dogs rather than children?"

"*Haba*, Mama, people also have children in America. Those who want children go to great lengths to have children—there are fertility clinics where people go for treatment. People even donate eggs and sperm so those who do not have can receive them and get pregnant."

"*Tufiakwa*, that is not the will of God; the best thing is to beg God for children. I am glad that you chose to listen to me and come back home to find a homegrown solution to your problem and not go to those fertility clinics," Ijeoma's mother-in-law said.

"But Mama, promise you'll at least come to visit us. You may find out you like the place."

"When you have your baby, I will definitely come to help you bathe and carry the baby. It will be worth the trip, and I look forward to that," her mother-in-law replied.

Shortly after Ijeoma got back to the United States, she discovered she was pregnant. At first she didn't believe it, but after two further tests, the result was the same. She was indeed pregnant. Juwah was excited and began to spend time away from the computer screen. Ijeoma would sometimes tell him to touch her stomach and feel the baby's movement. He would touch and squeal in delight like a child. They soon had a sonogram and found out it was going to be a baby girl. Both were delighted. They agreed that the baby's name would be Nnneka—"Mother Is Supreme."

When the baby was born, she was very fair, and a black birthmark almost covered one side of her rib cage. Ijeoma's mind went back to the little white fish with the black stripe. The doctor reassured her that the birthmark might fade away within a short time. The day after the baby was born, her color began to change to ink blue. She was having difficulty breathing. They hooked her up to an oxygen machine, but the baby did not get better, and later that night she died. An autopsy showed that the baby had been born with very underdeveloped, weak lungs.

Ijeoma called her mother-in-law and narrated the story of the death of Nnneka—Juwah's name for the baby, meaning "Mother Is Supreme"— all the while sobbing, with snot running down her nose. Her mother-in-law's response surprised her.

"Don't worry, at least the world now knows that you are not barren. You'll come home again. We shall return to the prophet's place. This time you'll pick a strong black fish, it'll be a boy, his lungs will be strong. . . ."

Ijeoma dropped the phone.

Stars in My Mother's Eyes, Stripes on My Back

Y ou are too slow; the pastor's wife has been waiting outside for close to ten minutes, we are going to be late for
church."

"Don't tell me I'm too slow. I have been the one doing all
the work, making breakfast and getting *your son* ready, and all
you've done is lie around, only for you now to tell me I'm too
slow, don't use that word again."

"Don't tell me what word to use and what word not to use. So
now I'm supposed to start cooking and bathing the child because
we are living in America, you stupid woman?"

"It is you who is stupid, not me; if you aren't stupid, you will
not call me stupid."

"It is your parents that are stupid, you useless and stupid
good-for-nothing woman. If you are not careful, we will not go
to church this morning. We'll stay home and dig it out, and by
the time I'm done with you, you will regret all the things coming
out of your mouth."

"Let's not go to church, I don't care. The only thing I regret in my life was ever meeting and marrying you, and my worst mistake was coming with you to America. Just look at me, what kind of life is this that I'm living, is this life?"

At this point my father stomped outside and with a tight smile on his face went and told the pastor's wife, who was waiting to give us a ride to church, that we were not coming. I heard the woman wave to him and drive away in her tomato red Ford truck. My heartbeat accelerated. Now they were truly going to have it out—if church was canceled for this quarrel, then they were going to have a go at it big-time. My heart sank.

"Open that dirty mouth of yours and talk to me again," Father said as he came back in, banging the door, the tight smile that had been on his face a few moments ago now gone.

"And what will you do if I open my mouth?"

"I will give you a dirty slap that you will never forget," Father said.

"Slap me, slap me," Mother screamed again and again, walking toward Father, her face contorted and dark. A gray-brown hue seemed to be floating in the whites of her eyes. And then he slapped her, not once, not twice, but three times, as viciously as I had seen him swat at a mosquito that had perched on him once at a picnic.

"You slapped me, now you have to kill me—you must kill me today and take my dead body back to my parents," Mother said, and began to wail aloud. But the slap soon began to take effect like a slow-acting drug, and she seemed to wilt and began to quake with heavy sobs.

"Get me the phone," she said to me.

As I walked toward the phone, Father's voice cut through to me.

"Leave that phone alone."

"I said bring me the phone, or are you deaf?" Mother screamed at me.

I hated to be caught in the middle this way; I hesitated and began to walk toward the phone.

"If you invite the cops and for any reason I am deported from this country, you will spend the remaining part of your stupid life in misery—in short, that is when you will really regret ever meeting me," Father said.

Mother went into the bathroom, lay down in the bathtub, and curled up like an infant in the womb.

Silence descended upon the days that followed, as it usually did. I became the go-between.

"Go and ask your father if he wants dinner," Mother would say to me, even though they were within hearing distance of each other.

"Tell your father that I need quarters to do the laundry."

"Tell your father that he has a phone call."

Father's response to these was never more than a grunt, and if the message involved money, with which to do the laundry for instance, he never gave any but cursed and asked aloud if Mother no longer had hands with which to wash the clothes. I went to school and came back each day hoping I would see them talking to each other, but this did not happen. This was unusual, because before now they usually made up within a few days.

One Friday evening, Uncle Boateng came to visit. Father fondly called him Boat and looked up to him in many ways. He was not really an uncle—he was Ghanaian, and we were Nigerian—but father insisted I call him Uncle. Though he had lived in America for over ten years, Uncle Boateng still spoke with a strong Ghanaian accent and wore kente-cloth shirts and a traditional woven African cap. He was a graduate student of physics and had been for ten years; he worked illegally as a distributor of the *Post-Standard* newspaper. He told stories about his job that made it sound like some glamorous occupation.

"The dogs in DeWitt and Fayetteville are the most wicked dogs in this country," he would say, laughing uproariously. "Ah, those dogs, they hide on the porch and the moment you come out of the car to drop off the paper in the box, they have reached you in one bound, and you know the worst part, they go straight for either your prick or your jugular, and the owners are right there behind the blinds, watching and smiling. As an illegal worker you are not covered by insurance, and if anything happens to you, you are on your own." He would then take Father to his old beat-up maroon Ford Taurus and show him the scratch marks made by dogs on the car's fading paintwork. Father took every word that came out of Uncle Boateng's mouth as the word of life.

"American boy," he called me as he entered the house with a bottle of vodka wrapped in a brown paper bag. He smiled at me, showing an expanse of pinkish red gums. It was a Sunday, and I was watching football on ABC; the picture quality was poor and the rabbit ears atop the television hung at a precarious angle.

"You should be watching real football, soccer as they call it here—you know, real African football, I mean by African superstars like Roger Milla of the Indomitable Lions of Cameroon, Jay Jay Okocha of the Nigerian Green Eagles, and Abedi Pele of the Black Stars of Ghana. And look, let me tell you something, the Americans are soon going to discover soccer, and then it will become big, and even now if you play well you can win a scholarship to Le Moyne."

Father came out of the study and greeted him. He stepped

back and looked at Father, gave him a once-over, and bellowed with laughter.

"You this man, look at how much weight you have lost because you had a minor quarrel with your wife, oh, so if you don't eat that *thing* for one month, you will die." He laughed again.

"And where is your wife? The woman that has made you lose all this weight, where is she, or can she tell me she did not hear my voice?" Mother came out of the room and genuflected in greeting. They all went into Father's study, and I returned to my football game. I could not concentrate on my game and soon went to take my accustomed position by the door. Uncle Boateng was talking to Mother.

"I know that it is tough for you, our women in this country. Staying at home all day, not working because of immigration rules, doing all the chores alone while the man is off to school, this useless school that we are attending at our old age. I know back home you'll have lots of people to help you with chores, but still you have to suffer now so that you can enjoy tomorrow."

"That is what I have been telling her all these years, but she would not listen," Father interjected.

"You, don't interrupt me when I'm speaking, I will soon get to you—or do you think you can bribe me not to speak the truth?" Uncle Boateng said to Father.

"Now, listen to me, woman, it is not for nothing that in Africa where we come from, the wife refers to her husband as 'the owner of my head.' We are in America, but still we are Africans, and you should not talk back to your husband, even more so in the presence of his first son."

"And as for you," he said, turning to my father, "you have to start changing; you cannot go through America without

America going through you. Even me, I'm changing; last Valentine's Day I took my wife out to a restaurant to eat just like Americans, I even bought her roses on her birthday. The rhythm of the drum has changed, and we the dancers have to change our dance steps. Now apologize to your husband. I do not want to come here to settle quarrels, I want to come here to celebrate the birth of a new baby."

I heard both Mother and Father laughing, and the sound of Mother's knees hitting the floorboards as she knelt down in apology. The door opened, Mother came out, and I ran back to my football game on television. I had missed a touchdown, and the commentators were still talking about it. The Orange men were getting back in the game.

Father came out to get the wine opener and saw Mother cutting up chicken to prepare pepper soup. Father looked at her and teasingly called her "stubborn woman."

"Ah, if I wasn't stubborn, you would have killed me, you *wicked* man," she said and they both laughed.

Soon the aroma of boiling chicken seasoned with garlic, basil, thyme, and curry and some African herbs that Mother usually bought from the African store on South Salina Street filled the apartment. I knew that the next day all the clothes in my closet would smell like curried chicken.

Highlife music was coming out of Father's study, and Uncle Boateng's laughter was booming. He and Father were talking and drinking and agreeing with everything the other said.

"Where is your son? He is almost a man now, and should be sitting here with us, drinking and picking up wisdom from sitting near his elders."

"Ah, do you want me to end up in jail, or don't you know that this is America?" Father said, and Uncle Boateng laughed again.

"Anyway, he can sit with us, can't he, there is no harm in that. At least there is no law yet saying he cannot sit with elders while they are drinking, or is there such a thing as secondhand drink, like you have secondhand smoke?" Uncle Boateng said, and they both laughed again.

I came and sat with them and pretended to be enjoying it while thinking of the football game on television.

"You are already a man, and according to the customs of our people back in Africa, you should by now be preparing to go into the bush and catch an animal with your bare hands and return with it to show the entire clan that you have become a man. But we are in America, and killing a squirrel here is an offense. So your father and I have been putting our heads together, and we have come up with an equivalent test of manhood for you," Uncle Boateng said.

Mother brought in the steaming bowls of pepper soup, and Uncle Boateng began to lick his lips. He grabbed a bowl from the tray, took a spoon, and began to drink the soup. I was worried the hot soup was going to scald his throat.

"Ah, you are looking at me with wonder—don't you know I have an air-conditioning unit inside my throat?" he asked, laughing. "Back home, when I was about your age, my parents sent me to a boarding school. That was where I learned to bolt down hot food. If you did not bolt down your food as soon as it was served, the senior prefects would start their endless announcements, and you could not eat while a prefect was speaking. By the time the prefect finished speaking, lunchtime was over and the food had to be poured away."

I too began to drink my bowl of soup, which had cooled somewhat since Uncle Boateng began telling his story.

WE ENTERED GALDI'S, the discount grocery store where Father preferred to do our grocery shopping. Buying groceries was a woman's chore back in Nigeria, but it was one duty Father did not find demeaning or complain about. When Mother used to shop for groceries, it was a source of endless quarrels between them. He would ask her for the receipt from her purchases and, his glasses perched precariously on his nose, hold a pencil in one hand while going through the receipts like homework. He would ask Mother lots of questions on a voided purchase, his eyebrows raised as he posed the question. He would rise from the dining table, still holding the receipt. Finally one day, Mother had blurted out that it was about time he started doing the grocery shopping himself, and Father had jumped at the offer as if it were a long-awaited opportunity.

Father inserted a quarter into the shopping cart and gestured for me to push the cart into the store.

"Pick whatever you like," he said to me. I could not believe my luck. Usually Father would frown when I asked if we could buy chocolates, yogurt, or breakfast cereals. His only concession was buying ninety-nine-cent bagels, nodding in my direction and saying, "I know you like bagels."

Galdi's was full today, and for some reason Father seemed to find this fact exciting. It was the typical Galdi's crowd of Sudanese and Croatian immigrants and poor old people who rode the Centro bus and closely examined every item they picked up from the shelf, put the same item back on the shelf, and then picked the same item up again and dropped it on another shelf.

I picked up a tub of ice cream, a few bars of chocolate, some cookies, and a giant pack of Mike and Ike. Father looked at me and asked if that was all I wanted. I began to pick up items at random, a six-pack of fruit jugs and about half a dozen different kinds of candy, but Father did not even stare at me. He bought the usual items that we needed—jumbo chicken thighs, tomato puree, pasta, vegetable oil, rice, and trash bags. Our shopping cart was overflowing at this point, but Father urged me to add a pack of Twinkies to my haul just before checkout.

There were four checkout lines, but Father picked carefully before we joined a line. He was sweating slightly, like someone at the verge of something, but I could not quite place whatever it was he had in mind. We began to off-load all our stuff onto the conveyor belt, with father smiling apologetically at a matronly white woman behind us. The cashier flashed us a false smile and began to tally our purchases. It came to a little over a hundred dollars. Father seemed genuinely surprised and pulled out a crumpled twenty-dollar bill and ten-dollar bill from his back pocket, all the while smiling at the woman behind us.

"I did not realize things have become this expensive, eh, I thought it was only the price of gas that has gone up," he said out loud and smiled at the cashier, but she did not return his smile.

"We have no choice, we cannot pay for your items, you have to return them." He began returning the items I had picked to the cashier, who asked, "You don't want these?" And without waiting for a response, she began to return the items to a cart near her. But the lady behind us on the line pulled Father aside and began to talk to him. I could hear her.

"I noticed you had to drop off a lot of stuff. See, I can help, and you don't have to pay me. I'm sure you would do it for someone else. I will pay the difference." She handed her debit card to the cashier and asked her to add the charge to her bill. Father seemed genuinely surprised and kept saying, "Thank you, thank you," in a voice that seemed not to be coming from him.

"It's not a problem at all, I'm sure you'll do it for somebody else, I used to have kids myself," the lady said and smiled, showing only her teeth.

We walked out of Galdi's loaded down like hunters with their kill. The traffic on Erie Boulevard pounded like African talking drums, and Father kept smiling and patting me on the back.

A Simple Case

"Your case is simple, you will soon be released," the sergeant said to Paiko. Paiko had been arrested earlier that evening during a police raid on Jolly Hotel, a brothel that harbored more than thirty female prostitutes.

In the late evening, Paiko was still sitting on a worn brown wooden seat behind the counter. He was beginning to get worried. His arrest was likely to stop him from going to his stall at the Alade Market, where he sold "Okrika Wake Up," imported secondhand clothes and bags. Since after his arrest, his girlfriend, Sweet, for whom he had been waiting to finish having sex with her last client so that they could go home together, had not yet come to visit him at the police station. He recalled a conversation he had had with Sweet a long time ago, when he first told her he wanted her to become his "special woman." She had smiled and told him that any man who wanted to keep an *ashewo*, a prostitute, as his woman must be prepared to catch the clap and should be ready to spend some time at the police station. He had been lucky until last night. Usually he would bribe the police whenever they came on a raid of the Jolly Hotel, but last night was different. The people who had arrested him were members of the newly formed SARS, Special Anti-Robbery Squad.

A new sergeant was taking over from the one who had been at the desk when Paiko was arrested. Paiko watched the new sergeant's face closely and smiled. He liked what he saw. The new sergeant had an overflowing belly, which was a good sign; he was likely to be a bribe taker.

"Don't worry, you'll soon be released—I am sure my colleague who is taking over from me will be the one to release you," the departing sergeant said to Paiko.

Paiko smiled nervously and said nothing. He was not too worried; this was a police post and not a fully fledged station. He suspected that no hardened criminals were in the cell, and the only smell that came from the cell was a faint odor of old urine. He was happy, however, that he was not in the cell.

The new sergeant cleared his throat, spat into a dusty corner of the room, and turned to Paiko.

"What is your offense, my friend?" Without pausing, he asked the same question in a different way. "What offense did you commit, mister?"

Paiko became worried; he thought the departed sergeant had briefed the new one on his case. He had seen them put their heads together while looking in his direction. Paiko summoned up some courage and smiled at the sergeant.

"I did not commit any offense, sir. I was arrested in a raid on Jolly Hotel," Paiko said.

"Then why do you say that you have committed no offense? Your being caught in a raid on a brothel is an offense—or do you want to lawyer me?" the sergeant asked, peering at Paiko through restless, bloodshot eyes. From where Paiko sat, he could smell the *ogogoro* vapors emitted by the sergeant.

"Oh, no, not at all, sir, I'm not trying to lawyer you at all, sir," Paiko said.

"Anyway, your case is a small matter; you will soon be released," the sergeant said, and began to read a sheaf of dog-eared soccer pools betting coupons.

Just then, the station radio came alive. The sergeant threw the frayed sheaf of coupons aside and snatched the radio. He saluted smartly, his huge belly jiggling like a water gourd.

"All correct, sah. I am the sergeant on duty, sah. What do you say? . . . An armed robbery along Ikorodu Road, a commissioner's official car snatched? Ah, that is very serious, sah."

Paiko watched as the sergeant began to twitch nervously, all the time scratching his large buttocks through his torn uniform, patched in three places.

"No problem, sah, we have enough of them here, you can come and pick them up with the Land Rover, there is no vehicle in our post. It is a small post, but we can provide you the men you need for the parade, no problem at all, sah."

The sergeant was suddenly transformed into a shouting, barking, wild-eyed creature.

"All of you criminals in the cell, form a line and start coming out of the cell with your hands raised in the air. If you try any monkey tricks with me, I will shoot you right away, and your family can come and collect your body in the mortuary."

He opened the door of the cell with a bunch of keys he picked up from a wooden board nailed to the wall. The men shambled out; there were six of them, all looking confused and bewildered. All the while Paiko had been sitting behind the counter, he had had no suspicion that the cell held such tough-looking men. The sergeant turned to Paiko and barked, "What are you doing there? Join the line—in fact you should be the first person in the line—and raise your hands in the air, or you will chop bullet right now."

"Ah, sir, I am not a criminal—you told me my case is simple, I told you I was arrested at Jolly Hotel," Paiko stammered.

The sergeant walked toward Paiko and gave him a slap across the face. Paiko blinked and blinked again, trying to dispel flashing stars.

"Now fall into the line before I waste you," the sergeant said. Paiko stumbled, his feet unsteady and his hands raised in the air like the other men.

An old police Land Rover arrived, and the sergeant led the men outside. An inspector with three broad tribal marks across both sides of his face jumped out, and the sergeant saluted him smartly.

"Are these the robbers?" he asked.

"Yes, sah, they are the armed robbers I told you about, sah."

"Why are they wearing all these clothes?"

"Sir, they were dressed like this when we arrested them at the scene of the crime, sah."

"You all, take off your trousers and your shirts, all of you, take them off quickly," the inspector said to Paiko and the rest of the men. Paiko was of a mind to tell the inspector that he was not an armed robber, but he changed his mind and decided to bide his time. The men removed their clothes and stood in their underwear, which was in various colors, sizes, and different states of disrepair. The sergeant commanded them to jump into the back of the Land Rover. He sensed some hesitation on their part. Pulling out a pistol, he raised it and shot into the air. Paiko threw himself into the back of the Land Rover, banging his head against the hard metal. As the smell of petrol filled his nose in the pitch-blackness of the vehicle, he began to cry like a baby. The vehicle pulled out of the station, and they were on their way to Area F, the state headquarters of the police command.

The men in the vehicle soon found their voices and began to talk in whispers.

"Where are they taking us to, sef?" a voice in the darkness asked.

"To Area F, now, their headquarters."

"Ah, Area F, is a bad place I tell you, that is one place I do not want to go to again. That is where they have the worst torture chamber in the whole of this country."

"But why are they taking us there?" another voice asked.

Paiko cleared his throat and spoke for the first time. He was listening to his own voice as the words came out, almost as if the words were not his; his mouth felt like an instrument that was separate from the rest of him.

"I heard the sergeant on the radio; he said some armed robbers snatched the official vehicle of a commissioner and that they needed to make a quick arrest. It was not long after he spoke on the radio that the inspector came."

"Ah, that means they are going to parade us as the armed robbers that snatched the commissioner's car. They told us to remove our clothes, so we'll look like the real robbers. We are even lucky that they did not shoot some of us in the leg—sometimes they do that to convince the public that the robbers were trying to escape or that it was a serious gun battle," a voice filled with experience said in the darkness.

"Area F torture chamber is the worst except for the Alagbon Close torture chamber at Force CID." The voice saying this seemed to be getting a lot of satisfaction from telling his tale.

"In Area F, they have large hooks in the ceiling. They tie the hands and legs of suspects like roast chickens. They hang them upside down and use heavy batons and *koboko* whips to wallop them all over their bodies and convince them to confess. If a person is proving stubborn and does not want to confess, they invite a popular sergeant there, his name is Sergeant Torture, and by the time he's done with you, you'll confess both the crimes you committed and the one you didn't," the same man said, chuckling to himself.

Paiko began to wonder why the man was doing this. He felt a warm trickle of sweat running down the crack to his anus. The same man cleared his throat and continued.

"Sergeant Torture will hold a suspect's penis in his hand and insert a rusty sharp bicycle spoke into it; sometimes if he does not want you to suffer too much he will use a sharp broomstick, ah, that place *na waya*," the speaker concluded.

The police Land Rover pulled into Area F. Before the vehicle could come to a proper stop, the inspector jumped out, and as the vehicle stopped, it was surrounded by men holding guns raised into the air. Some of them were wearing khaki shorts and black singlets and berets; others wore no shirts at all and were carelessly swinging their guns from side to side.

Area F had a peeling milky fence around it. Outside the fence hawkers held dripping plastic bags of sachet water for sale; a few hawked dead-looking loaves of bread and fried buns. After the vehicle stopped in the compound, Paiko and the other detainees were marched into the police station.

"You can take their statements later; these are dangerous criminals. They robbed the commissioner of his car. I am taking them straight into the cell," the inspector who brought Paiko and the others said to the corporal at the desk. He ordered Paiko and the other men to form a single line. With their arms raised they were marched into the cell.

The cell was a small room with a single lightbulb hanging very far away on the cement-decked ceiling; the floor was dark and grimy from urine, tears, sweat, and feces. Paiko could not see his way as he walked into the cell and stepped on someone lying on the floor.

"Who goes there, human beings or animals?" a raucous voice barked.

Paiko stepped gingerly away. As his eyes adjusted to the darkness of the cell, he began to see that at least three rings of men had formed circles. A tiny window on the far reaches of the wall, covered with three dark, rusty iron bars, was the only means through which air came into the cell. The heat was like that which emanated from the oven of a bakery. In one corner of the cell was a small pit latrine out of which thick vapors and a horrible stench emanated. The space around the pit latrine was cleared for the newcomers. The man who Paiko had stepped on was bleeding from a bullet wound; another man knelt beside him and was massaging a strong-smelling Chinese balm into the still fresh wound.

The same voice that had asked the question when the newcomers came in asked again, in a tone that was getting angrier, "Who goes there, human beings or animals?"

"Animals," answered the man who had been talking about the torture chambers on the ride down to Area F. The other voices answered, "Humans."

The man cleared his throat and laughed out loud. His laughter was clearly without humor, and as he laughed, the other people in the cell laughed along with him, except for the newcomers.

"I am the president of this cell, and I am known as Presido. This is Jungle Republic. There are no human beings here in Jungle Republic, we are all animals. The only people who are human beings are those living in the outside world—those of us in this inside world are all animals, *abi* my people no be true I talk?" he asked.

"True talk, Presido," the voices chorused.

"Just as you have your president and commander in chief in the outside world, I am the president and commander in chief in this Jungle Republic, even, *sef*, I have more powers than the president of this country, because if I want any one of you to die this very minute it will happen, no trial, no judge, *fiam*, like that you are dead."

"Up Presido!" the voices around the cell chorused. As Presido spoke, someone fanned him with a square piece of cardboard.

"Now, all of you line up according to your height and tell us why you should be admitted into this Jungle Republic," Presido said. The man who was behind Paiko nudged Paiko and whispered into his right ear; Paiko could smell the man's sour breath amid the general stench of the cell, an admixture of old cigarettes, marijuana, local gin, and decaying teeth.

"Tell them that you are a notorious armed robber, that you have led many operations and killed many people; they will fear you and give you an important position here in the cell," the man whispered. Paiko thought about this and shook his head. Something told him not to heed the man's advice. What he did not know was that the police sometimes locked up one of their own in the cell along with the criminals to help them gather information about robbers.

The man who had spoken to Paiko was the first to speak. He cleared his throat and launched forth boastfully.

"My name is Robert, but I am popularly known as Bob Risky. In the daytime I am a motor park tout at Iddo, but at night I am a robber. I have been robbing and killing since I was expelled from Mushin Grammar School in the second form for smoking and selling marijuana. There is no operation that is too risky for me to undertake—that is how I earned my nickname, Risky. I have been detained in almost all the police stations in Lagos, including Isokoko, Panti, Alagbon, Bar Beach, and even the old station on Malu Road. I was drinking in my girlfriend's beer parlor when the police raided the place and arrested me. They found a locally made pistol in my pocket, and some wraps of marijuana. When they are tired, they will release me. I have no other profession than armed robbery, and as we say, once a robber, always a robber." As Bob Risky finished his introduction, there was loud applause. Even Presido appeared to be impressed.

"You are one of us, and you are qualified to be a member of this republic. From today I make you the assistant provost of this republic. Your job is to maintain peace and law and order here and make sure that everybody stays in his position," Presido said. A cheer went up once again, and everyone in the cell hailed the new assistant provost.

Many people rose up to speak and talked about themselves and all their achievements in the world of armed robbery. One of them sang a song that he said a musician had composed in his honor. When it came to Paiko's turn, he became jittery. He opened his mouth to speak, but he only croaked. He swallowed the little saliva in his mouth and started again.

"My name is Paiko. I was drinking at Jolly Hotel while waiting for my girlfriend Sweet to finish entertaining a customer so we could go home together when the police raided the place and took me to Iloro police post. They told me my case was a simple one and that I would soon be released, but after some time the sergeant spoke with an inspector who told him that some people had robbed a commissioner of his car and that they needed people to parade as the robbers, and they put me in their Land Rover and brought me here," Paiko said and swallowed again.

"Ehheeen, so tell us the whole truth and nothing but the truth—were you drinking and waiting for your girlfriend Sweet after you returned from a robbery operation? Is she the one that helps you to hide your Luger? Tell us the truth and nothing but the truth," Presido said again, and the other voices in the cell echoed after him, "The truth and nothing but the truth."

"I am not a robber. I sell used clothing and handbags and shoes at the Alade Market, I am an honest man," Paiko said.

"Everybody in this cell is innocent until proven guilty, or is that not so?" Presido asked.

"We are all innocent until proven guilty," the voices in the cell repeated. Paiko did not know what made him do it, but he suddenly cleared his throat and began to tell them a story.

"One day I was in the open ground in front of the market when a customer came to me to buy a handbag. When she opened the handbag, she found two hundred dollars in shiny bills in the bag." At the mention of dollars, a sudden silence descended on the people in the cell. It was as if a foreigner with a different color of skin had walked in.

"Two hundred dollars, that is a lot of money—wait, let me convert it—that is roughly thirty thousand naira, *eehen*, so what happened?" Presido asked.

"This was not the first time I would find strange things in some of the clothes and bags that I sell. I would sometimes find lipsticks in handbags, sometimes condoms, love letters, a few coins, chaplets, and photographs."

"So what happened?" Presido asked.

"The woman, who was still haggling with me about the cost of the bag when she discovered the money, said the money was hers. I told her the money was not hers because we had not yet agreed on a price, and she had not paid me. I told her to give the bag to me, that I was no longer interested in selling, but she refused. We began to struggle for the bag, and a fight broke out."

"Stop right there," Presido said. "Jungle Republic legal adviser, where are you? Come out here and give us your advice." A wiry young man stepped forward. He was not a real lawyer but was known in the cell for his argumentative abilities. He gave advice and sometimes uninformed legal opinions to the detainees who were awaiting trial.

"Since they had not yet agreed on a price, and the woman had not paid for the bag, then she could not take the money; as a legal adviser, I make bold to say that there was an invitation to treat but an offer had not been agreed upon," the legal adviser said.

A voice suddenly began to speak from the rear end of the cell close to the open-pit latrine. "A man once bought a bottle of 7 Up for his girlfriend, who had come to visit him on a Sunday afternoon. It was during the 7 Up millionaire promotion—if you discovered any amount of money written on the crown of your soft drink, you won. The girl peeled the crown and discovered the amount of five hundred thousand naira written on the bottle crown. She told the man that the money belonged to her and not him," the voice said, enjoying the story.

"Who asked that man to speak? Did he raise his hand to ask permission before speaking?" Presido asked, sounding quite enraged. "Assistant Provost, help me give that foolish loudmouth three hot cups of tea."

The newly appointed assistant provost dragged the man out and delivered three very hot slaps to the man's face. "Now go close to the latrine and put your face there, *abi*—you think this is the outside world where there is no discipline and you people do whatever you like?" Presido commanded.

"*Eeeehen*, continue with your fine story, my innocent trader."

"The woman and myself were both taken before the leader of our market, Alhaja Isiwa. She gave the lady fifty dollars, fined me fifty dollars for fighting in the market, and gave me the remaining hundred dollars."

"So what did you do with the hundred dollars?" Presido asked.

"I gave half of the money to my girlfriend Sweet and invested the remaining fifty in my business."

"Your girlfriend must have given you special service that night, eh," Presido said smiling.

"She kissed the money, placed it on her breast, and told me that one day she too will start earning dollars."

"That your girlfriend, *sef*, don't forget that a beautiful woman is like delicious soup, everyone wants to get a taste of it. Now tell me, does your market leader know that you are here?"

"No, I have not been able to call anybody since I was arrested," Paiko said.

"I will help you—you are a good hardworking man, and you are a good storyteller. Someone call the corporal on duty and tell him we want to hire his cell phone," Presido said.

PAIKO WAS ABLE to get through to Alhaja Isiwa, and she raised money from other traders at the Alade Market and used her influence to bribe the police. Paiko was released after a few days and went back home.

All the while that Paiko was in the cell, he had been thinking of Sweet and why she had not bothered to come and see him, and what he was going to tell her when he set his eyes on her. The evening after his release, he took a shower, dressed up, and went down to the Jolly Hotel. He ordered a bottle of Star lager beer and sat on a stool sipping it slowly as he waited for Sweet to come out and wrap her soft, sweaty hands around his eyes, a game that they often played.

"Where is Sweet?" Paiko asked the barman.

"Ah, you have not heard?" the barman asked.

"Heard what? Did something happen to her?" Paiko asked.

"Yes, something good happened to her—she has gone to Italy."

"To Italy—what has she gone to do in Italy?"

"What else? *Haba*, are you not living in this country? She has gone to continue the business she was doing here and earn dollars."

"When did she leave?" Paiko asked.

"The day after our hotel was raided by policemen," the

barman said. "But don't worry, women come and women go, but Jolly Hotel remains. There is a new girl that has just arrived, her name is Beauty and she is a real sweet sixteen. Should I go and call her for you?"

Paiko did not respond. He remembered when he had handed the fifty-dollar note to Sweet, and she had kissed it and placed the money on her breast and said one day she too would start earning dollars. He had assumed that she meant that she would start going to nightclubs and dating the expatriate oil workers. He recalled what Presido had said in Jungle Republic about a beautiful woman being like delicious soup, and everyone wanting a taste. He took a sip of his beer and turned to the barman.

"Call that new girl for me."

Welcome to America

When I first came to America to attend graduate school I lived in what was considered a rough neighborhood, but I did not know it then. Having recently arrived from Africa, I had seen images of hoodie-wearing, gun-carrying figures on television and assumed my neighbors were the normal people one expected to see in America. We lived in an old hotel, built probably in the 1960s but now converted into one-bedroom apartments and efficiencies. Because you could sign a three-month lease with those who managed the apartments, a large number of the people who lived in the apartment block were transients. There were also a few international students from Asia.

In my early days in the building, I would occasionally see a bespectacled Asian-looking girl wandering around the countless dark passageways. I would sometimes smile at her in the tight lip-twitch style favored by the Americans who passed me on the street. Was it possible that the bespectacled lady was actually the ghost of a female student from Asia who had lived in the apartment next to mine a few years back? Her story had

been told to me by an African student from Kenya who lived in
the same building.

She was pursuing graduate studies and had also been a teaching assistant, just like me. Her mostly young white American
students gave her a hard time in class. Her accent stood in the
way of her teaching, and her students spent all her teaching time
correcting her pronunciation of common words. She would
come back to the apartment weeping. In addition to her problem
with her students, she had an equally hard time understanding
her professors and would go to class with a midget tape recorder
with which she recorded her lectures. She would spend the night
trying to transcribe the tapes—rewind, transcribe, rewind, transcribe . . . until she fell asleep on the kitchen table where she
studied. When she stood before her students the next day to
teach, her nerves shot to pieces and her raw eyes hidden by her
glasses, she would become nervous, and her words would run
together, making her accent worse. At the end of the semester
she performed very poorly, and because of this, coupled with her
students' horrible evaluations, the university asked her to leave.
She had been shattered. She came back to her apartment and
hanged herself. Was it possible that her ghost was wandering the
poorly lit passageways?

The man who lived next door to me smoked marijuana; the
smoke floated into my apartment as I lay on the couch studying. The quantity of smoke was so great, I would become stoned
merely from inhaling the secondhand smoke and doze off on the
couch. My wife would lift me and carry me to the bedroom.

While I was growing up in Nigeria, one of my uncles, an
ex-soldier, had a large marijuana farm. On occasion when we
visited the farm we would see snakes, antelopes, and cane rats

lying around the farm, happily stoned from eating the marijuana leaves and seeds. We would pick them up and take them home to cook them in the pot. Every time my wife carried me into the bedroom, I felt like those animals.

This same neighbor who smoked marijuana would knock on my door every other day to borrow bathroom tissue, a dollar, or ice cubes. I had once foolishly offered him a bottle of beer; every evening after that he would he would knock on my door and ask me, "Say, yo' still got some of that wonderful beer you gave me the other night?" One cold winter night I came back from classes and found the entire apartment block cordoned off by police. My wife and daughter were standing outside. The police had come to arrest him for a burglary at the nearby shopping center for which he was a prime suspect. When the police knocked on his door, he told them to leave because he had twelve kinds of guns on him. The entire apartment block was evacuated. He screamed at the police for hours and then became silent. Finally, a member of the Special Forces had gone in through the ceiling. They found him lying on his bed, stoned and sleeping. He went to jail and would write me begging letters, asking for a ten-dollar loan.

The building next to us was occupied by a motley crowd, middle-aged men and women who sat on camp chairs all day, smiling vaguely and smoking. My daughter would wave to them from my kitchen window, and they would wave back at her and ask her to come over. She was two years old at the time and enjoyed playing with people's glasses and touching long curly hair. We would let her go and join them sometimes, and she would come back home smelling of smoke and loaded down with candy. My wife and I speculated about who they were. She said they must be members of a religious cult, since they all lived together. I told her that they were likely to be relations living in their family's house. In the early 1940s in Nigeria, my grandfather had made his fortune from being the sole distributor of Crocodile machetes. From the money he made, he had built a four-story house on the mainland part of Lagos, which became known as the family house. The house was occupied by all kinds of distant relations—uncles, cousins, no matter how distantly removed they were from us. Our people who lived in the village would wake up one morning and pick up their bags and start heading for Lagos. When asked where they would stay, they would mention the family house. And indeed, whenever they arrived, room was found for them. If they were young enough, my grandfather would take them to his sprawling machete store to work as attendants.

While growing up, I spent all my summer holidays in the family house. My grandfather insisted that all his grandchildren should spend their long summer vacation in the family house. Our parents would drop us off, and we would change into *buba* and *sokoto* made from local cotton fabrics. None of my relations who lived in the house spoke English, so we learned to speak the vernacular. By going to the shop, we also learned to haggle and count money. Grandfather's rule was that all the children should eat from the same large basin. At mealtimes, we all dipped our hands into the same plate, from the oldest to the youngest, and if you did not grab enough, well, too bad. It was one of the first houses to have a television set. Children and adults would stand by the mosquito netting on the window and peer at the screen in the living room. "How did they get them into the box?" they would ask nobody in particular. Grandfather told us that when he first bought his large radiogram, a neighbor who had come to visit had sat listening to the voices on it for a long time. Finally summoning courage, he had asked Grandfather, "These people in the box who talk all day and are always happy and singing and dancing, what do they eat?" "Eggs," Grandfather replied. From that day on, the neighbor would bring a basket of eggs to Grandpa and whisper into his ears, "For the people in the box."

It was many years later that I came to know that the occupants of that house next to us were not the members of a family in the sense in which I knew it. It was what was referred to as a halfway house, a house for drug addicts in recovery. The twitches that my wife had mistaken for religious ecstasy were actually the jouncing of addicts suffering withdrawal symptoms.

On the other side of the old hotel lived an old woman who looked a hundred years old. Her name was Jane Kelly. She loved my daughter and would tell me that her Jim would really love my daughter when he visited. She said she was expecting him to come home from the hospital during Thanksgiving. Jim was her husband, who had passed away ten years ago. She would grab my hands and ask me to tell her stories about Africa. "I love animals," she would whisper, "tell me about giraffes and tigers and lions." I could not tell her that the only time I had seen a lion was at the university zoo. This lion at the university zoo would become famous years later when it ate a man who called himself Pastor Daniel. The self-styled pastor had prayed and fasted for forty days and had gone to the lion's den with his followers to prove to them that he was like the biblical Daniel. The lion had of course eaten him. The lion's picture made the front page of the national dailies the next day.

One day, as we sat in Jane Kelly's apartment, looking out her window, we saw two black squirrels running on the telephone lines. I turned to her and said, "Squirrels are enjoying American freedom—where I come from, some people trap them and eat them."

"Say that again," she said, turning her ears to my mouth.

"The squirrels are enjoying American freedom," I said; she grabbed my hands and laughed out loud, stamping her thin legs on the wooden floorboards. Thereafter each time I visited, she would grab my hands with her soft small hands and scream, "Squirrels are enjoying American freedom!" Her apartment was filled with all manner of knickknacks, and she always had a gift for my daughter. No matter how much I tried to convince her to the contrary, she would always turn to me and say in sympathy, "There is a war going on in Africa, right?" I stopped trying to convince her after some time. She had a home aide who came in to take care of her. After some time she could no longer afford to pay the aide and was moved to a nursing home. I never saw her again. But whenever my daughter saw a white-haired old woman, she would point and scream, "Jane, Jane!"

That first winter, I came down with what I thought was malaria but which actually turned out to be the flu. I lay on the couch, my eyes and nose running and my body fluctuating between extreme cold and extreme heat. I did not yet know the procedure for getting a personal physician, and every time my daughter was feeling unwell, my wife would give her a spoon of gripe water. I lay on the couch and suffered. I recalled two incidents from my childhood. While growing up, my father had befriended an American Christian missionary. His name was Charles Nathan. He preached a strange doctrine: he said life was going to end on earth very soon. He was rumored to have raised a man from the dead. His mission was to organize crusades and revivals to warn souls about the impending destruction of the earth. The day before his crusade, he came down with a fever. He was sweating so much the mattress on which he lay was soaked through and his sweat formed a pool on the floor. Beside him lay his fat black Bible and film slides titled "The Photodrama of Creation." He babbled in a strange tongue and tossed from side to side. He had to be rushed to the general hospital, and when he recovered, he canceled his crusade and went back to America. He had contracted a rare form of cerebral malaria. As I lay on the couch, I wondered whether my fate was not going to parallel that of Pastor Charles Nathan. Would I be forced to cancel my studies and return to Nigeria? My wife bought herbal tea from a Chinese shop down the road and plucked guava and mango leaves from the trees on campus. She boiled these in a large pot. She brought the pot to where I lay on the couch and asked me to sit up. She placed the steaming pot in front of me and covered me with two thick comforters. I sat under the comforters sweating until the fever broke. Looking back on this incident now, I smile. I was being treated with the same methods that old herbalists from interior villages used to cure rheumatism and malaria in Africa, even though I was living in one of the most advanced countries in the world. For days I was weak, and my hands flapped beside me lifelessly. Could I have come all the way to America to be felled by the common flu? I recovered, and that illness may have marked the beginning of the end of my period of innocence.

I came to realize, for instance, that the emergency exit door that was always open no matter how many times I closed it was the door through which those who came to buy crack passed.

The guy who would smile at me each time I closed the door and would watch me get into my room and then open it again was a dope dealer. He in fact was armed all the time he smiled at me and puffed at his Newport cigarettes.

The man who began to open my eyes to my environment was Mike, a Palestinian who ran a neighborhood store. I would always go to his store to buy black-eyed peas, and he would smile at me.

"Where are you from?" he asked me one day.

"Nigeria," I responded.

"Oh, no wonder you are so respectful. I'm from Palestine, you know, the old country. We too respect older people, but this is America, and there is no respect here, the young girls talk to you from their waist."

"Yes, we respect older people in my country," I said.

"In Palestine, when a lady enters a bus you get up for her, but me, here I don't get up for anybody, because there are no ladies."

"Well—," I said.

"Where do you live?" he asked me.

"I live down the road, the old hotel."

"You gotta be careful there; it is filled with no-good people nowadays. In the old days, when it was managed by Tom Walker, it was one of the best apartment buildings," he said. He was the one who told me that the house next to mine was a halfway house, and that the occupants were drug addicts in recovery.

"This is a great country, you know, it takes care of everybody. When I was living in Palestine, my younger brother began to run with the wrong gang and started smoking hashish. My father— a very strong man, I'm like him, you know—he tied my brother up, he trussed him up like a goat and threw him into a dark storeroom behind the house. He stayed there screaming for days. No food, no water, for thirty-nine days. When he came out, he was sober. No more hashish. My brother, he lives in Delaware now with his wife and children, he owns his own store just like me. But here, they put them in a halfway house and feed them for free. I sometimes wish I was an addict," he said, smiling.

After we moved and enrolled my daughter in preschool, the school district sent us a letter containing the names of child molesters on their watch list. Two of the names were people we had lived with in the apartment building. One of them, a kind-looking old man, had seen me in the lobby once and asked me if the child with me was my daughter, and when I told him yes, he had remarked that she was precious. He had asked my permission to get her a piece of candy from the vending machine, to which I had agreed.

Our new building was called the St. Leo Apartments. It lacked some of the colorful characters in our previous apartment block. But it was more expensive as well. After living for some years now in America, I still consider those innocent years in the old apartment building as the happiest days of our lives.

Teeth

The husband was home when the pains came. It was a drizzling fall evening. The doctor had told them to start coming to the hospital when the contractions became regular. They called a cab, and she cried all the way to the hospital. He thought she was in a lot of pain, but she told him later that she had cried because back home, when a woman was to have a baby, the men sat outside drinking *ogogoro*, the local gin, while the woman was surrounded by local midwives and aunts and cousins and grandmothers who had had many children themselves and knew how to flip the baby in the womb if it chose to come feetfirst instead of headfirst.

It was the wife's idea that they should have a baby while in America. He was not very enthusiastic about the idea; he was here to study, he told her. And, besides, babies cried a lot, and one of the things that was said about white people when he was growing up in Nigeria was that they did not like noise, the other two being that (1) they did not tell lies, and (2) they were completely fearless. Since they came to America, he had added reason to agree with the fact that white people did not like noise. The tiny apartment where they lived was always deathly quiet. They had had a long argument, keeping their voices down. He could not tell the wife that his classes were not going so well. He could hardly follow the speech of the professors. Their language was very idiomatic; they and the students had common terms of reference that he lacked. Sometimes in class, the professor and everyone else would be laughing. He would have his head buried in his notebook, not even knowing a joke had been made.

"Every child born on American soil is an American citizen," she told him. The husband did not know that citizenship was automatic. He thought it was something the child got after living for a certain number of years on American soil and meeting certain eligibility requirements. "And any child born here can become the president of this country." Can you imagine that, their child a president of the most powerful country in the world? He could imagine it himself, seeing his grandmother and all his relations from Nigeria with colorful loincloths around their waists lounging on the beautiful green lawn of the White House. She told him about the Kenyan whose father had been an international student just like him when he was born. She told him he was now a senator, and that his Kenyan relatives told the *New York Times* that they had danced through the night when they heard the news that he had been elected a senator.

"But that is not even the best part—the best part is that when our son is eighteen, he can file for a green card for us, his parents, to join him here in America, and you know what that means, it means we can spend our old age in this beautiful country."

He did not know that either. He sometimes wondered about all the things she knew about the country. The country puzzled him more by the day. None of his assumptions held. He was constantly in a state of bewilderment and would open his mouth to gulp in air each time he was shocked or surprised. Since he was puzzled all the time, his mouth was perpetually open.

What he did not tell the wife was that lovemaking was not at the top of his list anymore. He had tried to reason through it, why it no longer meant anything to him, but he couldn't be sure. He sometimes reasoned it was the half-naked girls that he saw on campus every day. It had shocked him at first, but after some time he had gotten used to them. He sometimes told himself his lack of interest in sex was a result of the cold. The winter in upstate New York that year had been the worst in ten years. He would come in from campus after walking one and a half miles in the snow, his eyes red, his face frozen, even the snot in his nostrils frozen stiff.

He would stay in the sitting room, pretending to be reading, while the wife got ready for bed. She would look at him and go to bed while he sat in the sitting room reading the same line a hundred times; and he would sleep on the couch when he got tired.

Sometimes the wife told him she had learned some new things about lovemaking from the shows she watched on television. This bit of news perked him up and made him leave the couch and go to the bedroom. She was right; she had indeed learned new things.

He did not believe her when she said she was pregnant. He still imagined that it had to be done in a certain position for at least a dozen times. He took her to the university health center. The nurse practitioner, who smiled all the time, ran a test for her, and within five minutes confirmed that she was indeed pregnant.

She also told them that in a few months' time they could have a
sonogram to determine the sex of the baby, like most couples did
in America. But his wife, who otherwise embraced everything
American, objected to that.

"We don't do that in Africa," she told the nurse.

The wife then went into a long analogy about how babies
were like parcels that had been handed to us, and sonograms
were like peeking at the parcel on the way home to find out what
its contents were instead of waiting to get home to find out what
it contained in the privacy of your house.

"It is your decision, and I respect it," the nurse practitioner
had told them. This was one of those American expressions that
baffled him—he encountered them every day, and they transformed conversations into legal expressions.

The wife saw it differently; she was happy. She thought the
nurse practitioner was a nice person and had a lot of respect for
Africans. She added it to the list of things that made America
such a strange country. She added it to the list of things she told
her mother on the phone each time she made those long-distance
calls back home. Those conversations that always began, "Hmm,
these people are very strange, you know; can you imagine that
criminals must be read their rights and told to remain silent
while being arrested, you know, unlike our own policemen that
would let you say incriminating things about yourself so as to
get you into more trouble. Hmm, do you know that if your husband lays his hands on you here, you could have him arrested?
Our uncle Zanza, who beats his wife on the thirtieth of every
month when he collects and drinks away his wages, should come
here. Hmm, do you know there are couples here who choose not
to have babies so that they can enjoy each other more?"

She would hear her mother's angry hiss from the other end of the telephone line.

"And they call that life?" her mother would ask.

The nurse had also told them to announce to their friends that they were having a baby, which was yet another strange American practice. In their part of the world, you did not need to tell people. You waited till they could see with their eyes that you were pregnant. Little wonder there were many proverbs about pregnancy, one of which was that it was like smoke, and could not be hidden. Another proverb had it that pregnancy was Nature's way of telling the world not to trust women with secrets.

The pregnancy gave her something to do. She now had doctor's appointments and lab appointments and was able to leave the house, unlike before, when she spent all her time indoors watching daytime soaps and talk shows. The doctor gave her a note to the county office, and she was given coupons for milk and tuna and carrots.

"See, we are already reaping the rewards of an American baby," she told her husband as she brandished the coupons.

They debated what she should do in case the pains started while he was away on campus. He gave her twenty dollars and told her to keep it somewhere safe and to call a cab if the pains began while he was away on campus. She told him that American men held their wives' hands while they had their babies. He smiled and told her to watch less television.

Now he sat on a chair by the labor room as morbid thoughts ran through his mind. He was more worried about the fact that she could die while having the baby than anything else. The school made international students take out an insurance policy for themselves and their spouses that would cover the cost of taking their bodies home in case they died.

He heard his wife's cry and then the cry of the baby and a brief silence and then only the cry of the baby. He walked to the door and waited. The doctor came out and beckoned to him; he was frowning slightly.

"What is wrong? Is she dead?" he asked.

"Mother and baby are fine. Please come in, we want you to take a look at something."

He walked in, his feet feeling as if his shoes were made of heavy steel. He saw that his wife was alive; she looked at him and gave him a small smile.

"He is very dark, just like you," she said, smiling wanly. What had she expected, that the baby would be white, because they lived among many white people?

"It is very unusual, just take a look at this," the doctor said, lifting the new baby's upper lip.

He peered into the little mouth; the baby had a full set of teeth. He grabbed the doctor's hands; the nurses and attendants were looking up to him like he held the answer and all he needed to do was open his mouth and give them a logical explanation. The father was frightened.

Back in Nigeria, the elders would have consulted the oracle so they could know what this meant. He did not imagine this kind of thing would happen here. He would have been less shocked if the baby had been a curly blond or an albino. He turned to the doctor.

"How did this happen?" he asked.

The doctor gently removed his hands from the father's and assumed a professional manner.

"Otherwise he is a perfect baby, and very long for a child too. You just might have a basketball player in the family."

He looked at the doctor and looked at the bloodstained sheets surrounding them and began to weep. His wife too, as if she had been waiting for this cue, began to cry.

"There are options, I mean. We have run a battery of tests and all that, and we still plan to do more, but I just thought I should ask you, since you people are not from the United States and all, is this common where you come from? We were wondering whether it was cultural. No doubt it is a medical mystery. I have heard that in some parts of the world people are born with only two toes; at the university hospital up the hill, an African woman had this lovely baby with six fingers and six toes. I do not mean to embarrass you; I feel you may be able to offer some kind of explanation. . . ."

The doctor trailed off.

He had hardly heard what the doctor said. His mouth felt dry, and he gulped in air, feeling suffocated. The nurses began to clean up. One of the nurses was talking to his wife about breast-feeding. It appeared that everything had once again returned to normal.

The hospital staff were furtive in their dealings with the husband and wife; they could hear people whispering in the large hallway about the strange African baby. The husband was afraid; he told the wife that he had heard on television that the government took away strange babies to secret laboratories in the desert where they put them in glass boxes like tropical butterflies and studied them. While they were talking, a woman with a camera came in. She was smiling.

"Hello, mom and dad. Can I take a picture of the baby?"

"Are you from the newspaper?" the woman asked, clutching the baby tightly to her chest.

"No, actually I work for the hospital. We need the baby's photograph for our records and our Web site."

"Do we have to pay?" the man asked, regaining his voice.

"No, it is absolutely free," the female photographer said, and repeated the word "free."

"What is the baby's name?" she asked.

"He has no name yet," the husband said. "In our part of Africa you don't give a new baby a name until the seventh day."

"How neat," the female photographer said and began to position her camera. She touched the baby's cheeks to get a smile. The baby smiled, showing his teeth; the photographer's face reddened, and she very nearly dropped the camera.

"Oh my goodness, I never saw—oh my goodness," she said again and began to snap away feverishly, the popping flashbulb brightening the room and temporarily blinding the husband and wife.

"You've got a long one there too," she said as she detached the flashbulb from her camera and started putting it away.

The husband shared the food the hospital provided for the wife. The wife urged him to eat: "You know I am not home, and there is no one to make your food."

The husband urged her to eat, telling her that she needed to eat well to breast-feed the baby. The baby began to cry; the woman picked him up and began to breast-feed him.

"Thank God it is producing milk; the nurse told me that for some women it took a couple of days before they began to produce milk."

"Does he bite you with it?" the man asked.

"No, he is just sucking away. I don't feel anything. He must be very hungry."

"Come and take a look," she said, raising his blanket and pointing at the baby's stomach. Half a dozen fine lines ran from one side of the tiny stomach to the other.

"Remember, the doctor said he was going to be a basketball player—see, the lines must have come from his curling himself up so tightly in that little space."

"What are we going to do with that?" the husband said, pointing at the drooping bit of navel from the umbilical cord.

"Don't worry, it will fall off in a couple of weeks."

"I mean, where are we going to bury it when it falls off? Or do you mean you don't know that back home you are buried wherever that bit of navel is buried?"

"Oh, yes, that—when it falls off, I will keep it at the bottom of my box where I keep my clothes and preserve it with camphor. We can take it back with us whenever we are going back home."

The husband did not respond. His head fell back on the hospital chair, and his mind went back to his childhood.

He was sitting by his grandmother's feet, and she was telling him a story; it was something that happened in the land of Idunoba. The inhabitants of Idunoba were dying of thirst. They woke up one morning and discovered that a black python had taken over the well that was the community's only source of water. All the brave hunters who went to the well to kill the python ended up being strangled by it. Then a woman who had been pregnant for seven years began to feel birth pangs. The baby came into the world feetfirst. When he opened his mouth, he had a complete set of teeth, and he used this to bite off his umbilical cord. While everyone in Idunoba watched, he began to grow. His arms became stout, and his feet grew sturdy, and he stood at over seven feet. He began to speak and command the villagers to take him to the well. When he got to the well, he used his bare hands to drag out the python and choked it to death. Everyone was happy, including the king. He gave the boy his daughter to marry, and they had seven brave sons and lived happily ever after.

Now the wife was shaking the husband and asking him to wake up so he could go home. She had assumed he was sleeping. He rubbed his face, picked up his bag, and left.

When he got home, he assembled the new crib that he bought for the baby from Kmart and hung up a balloon on the doorway that said "Congratulations."

The next morning he went to the hospital to bring the baby and mother back home. The wife had called him the previous night to tell him that the doctor had confirmed that all the tests were negative, and she was free to go home. The doctor told her to clean the baby's teeth with cotton wool and warm water.

There was a bit of a situation when they were about to leave the hospital. The state law required all newborn babies to be transported in an infant car seat. They did not have a car, so they didn't have a car seat. The hospital loaned them one, and they took a taxi back home.

The wife was happy on seeing the balloon when they entered their apartment, and thanked him. She was happy because he was becoming American in his ways. She put the baby in the crib, and he continued the sleep he had started at the hospital. The woman told him she was tired, went to bed, and dozed off. He read for a while and also fell asleep. The baby woke up twice in the night and was suckled by the wife.

The child continued to grow, and when he was a few months old, they bought him a toothbrush. Just because he had teeth, they gave him meat to chew on occasion, but he always spat it out.

The hospital sent a social worker to visit them to find out if they needed any assistance. The wife became friendly with the social worker, and it was the social worker that told her that here in America, people believed in something called the tooth fairy.

"You'll see, when your son grows up and starts school, he will learn about the tooth fairy."

The wife was happy to hear this little piece of news, and when the husband came back from school, she shared it with him.

"This means they are not so different from us," the wife said.

"Yes, they are not so different," the man agreed.

"I told my mother about it," the wife said.

"I thought we agreed you were not going to tell her," he said.

"I could not bear it anymore; I had to tell her."

"And what did she say?"

"She said it is a sign of greatness—she said her grandson is going to be a great man."

"For once I agree with your mother," the husband said, and looked at the wife with mischief lurking at the corners of his mouth.

They both began to laugh. Their laughter woke up the baby, who was taking a nap, and he began to cry.

An Incident at Pat's Bar

The bars favored by American oil workers in Port Harcourt were named after girls—retired prostitutes called club girls. The names were short and memorable—Pat's Bar, Stella's Bar, Abby's Bar, Christy's Bar, and so on. The oldest of them was Pat's Bar; it was also the one most visited by the older oil workers. You could tell the older oil workers by the color of their skin, a very dark brown like the color of anthills. You could spot the old-timers: they smoked Marlboro Reds, were usually potbellied like most of the prosperous locals, and had their shirts unbuttoned to the chest, revealing wiry gray chest hairs. They spoke a smattering of pidgin English, sprinkled with local expressions such as *wahala*, *oga*, *ashewo*, *nyash*, and *na wah*.

The girls had been given money to open the bars as gifts from departing boyfriends. Pat's was a parting gift from a boyfriend who had returned to Texas. Over the years the place had grown into the favorite hangout of old expatriate oil workers. Pat openly cultivated these oil workers, making trips to the interior to bring young girls from Opobo and Nembe for her customers, who preferred them very young.

She would tell the other women so everyone could hear it, "All of us are club girls o, every girl who runs a bar in this Port Harcourt na ashewo, we be all prostitutes from A to Z, we know ourself o, make nobody deceive herself we all slept with oyibo to get money, so why I no permit young girls wey want to hustle and make money like me." You could tell how prosperous she had grown from the folds on her neck. Her community had even conferred a chieftaincy title on her, Chirizua—"Uplifter of the Youths."

Pat's Bar was one of the few places where male prostitutes hung out to be picked up by expatriates. It also had a couple of decent rooms upstairs for "fresh fish," the slang for newly arrived expatriate oil workers who had yet to find permanent accommodation. When these expatriates became well established in Port Harcourt, they never forgot the early days when they were still finding their feet, and Pat's hospitality to them. The bar had cheeseburgers and fries, reminding its American patrons of home food. It also had several varieties of mustard and imported Heinz ketchup, not the tart-tasting locally made variety to be found at Christy's Bar four blocks down the road. When you changed your money in the informal *bureau de change* at Pat's Bar, you were sure you were getting genuine and clean naira notes, not the mutilated and sometimes counterfeit notes that were mixed with the real notes when you changed at Hotel Presidential.

Every year Pat adopted a local charity, and she kept a transparent plastic box for collecting donations on a stool in the bar. The first year she did this for St. Anne's Motherless Babies'

Home, she collected close to two hundred thousand naira when the money was converted into the local currency. The local catechist and his wife who ran the orphanage could not believe their eyes when they saw the money, and from that day on, they designated a special seat for her in the church. Different charities began to approach her to put a box for them in her bar. She would look at a soliciting pastor, shake her head, and smile.

"But you are the same people that criticize prostitutes in your church. Na una talk say na ashewo work we dey do for here, when una reach church on Sunday na to siddon for pulpit dey take mouth scatter us say na we dey corrupt this town of Port Harcourt." The pastor would bow his head sheepishly as she carried on her tirade.

"Una don forget say even for Bible, sef, God say judge not so that nobody go judge you, even Rahab in the Bible was a prostitute."

She would relent after her tirade, set up a box for the charity, and by the end of the year would have a large sum of money. The expatriates were always happy to drop a couple of dollars to help motherless children, especially after a night of heavy drinking and with one of Pat's girls hanging on their arm.

Her fish pepper soup was the best in town. She had two fishponds filled with live catfish; all a customer needed to do was point, and the fish was quickly brought out of the pond and killed.

There was no kind of drink that was not sold in the bar, from the local Gulder and Star lagers to Heineken, Budweiser, Michelob, and Guinness, and of course the house specialty, nicknamed Monkey Tail by the expatriates, a potent mixture of local rum, marijuana, and seven pieces of alligator pepper. It was rumored that when one of the American expatriates, Chet Williams, had first arrived in the country, he had taken more than the recommended one shot and ended up with a hangover that lasted for seven days. As he lay on the floor, writhing and yelling for ice water, he claimed that he saw snakes crawling all over the floor.

Pat got people out of all kinds of trouble, ranging from traffic infractions to separating them from local girls who had become too clingy. She had recently intervened when was one of her girls had become pregnant and refused to abort because she wanted to have a child with fair hair and blue eyes like engineer Rogers, her expatriate boyfriend.

It wasn't that there were no other good places to drink, but Pat's Bar, with its New York Yankees vest and cap in a glass frame, blown-up pictures of Madonna and Marilyn Monroe, and American quarters and cents glued to the bar, felt like home to most of the oil workers.

There were other places—the Shell Club, the Hotel Presidential Bar, and the Metropolitan Club 1938—that were frequented by British expatriates. These were places where you could drink your beer in peace, without a thin girl with pale skin and a false American accent brushing up against you and asking if she could share your seat or drink. Pat's patrons considered these other places sterile and antiseptic.

Those who drank at Pat's Bar knew what they were looking for, and there was plenty of that. Within the bar's confines, you could talk about how the locals crossed the road like goats without looking left or right, and you need not look over your shoulder to see if someone was listening. You could throw up right there at the bar, and the unobtrusive barman would clean you up and take you upstairs to lie down for a bit to clear your head. The expatriates would point at the hand-lettered sign on the white fence outside that said DO NOT UNIRET HERE, OKADA NO PARKING DROP AND GO and laugh out loud. Pat had deliberately refused to correct the spelling errors when she discovered that her customers were fascinated by them. Yet the bar was never rowdy. The girls behaved themselves, and a few expatriates had been heard to remark that Pat ran a tight ship.

It was not that locals did not want to come there to drink, but somehow they could tell that they were not welcome. The beer cost almost ten times what it did in the local bars, and the girls would hiss at any local who called to them.

"Shuo why are you calling me, abi monkey no sabi him mate again, please ants move with ants and crickets move with crickets, abeg na oyibo I dey follow o I no dey follow you Port Harcourt men, fuck no pay thank you very much. Or you think because God gave me my thing free I should give it free to any man with a penis."

Even the musician who played on Friday nights, who used to be known as Prince Shagasha, changed his name to Kenny Rogers Junior in order to please his clients and stopped singing African highlife, switching to country and western.

There were two categories of patrons at Pat's Bar, those who lived in Port Harcourt and those who worked offshore. The latter category was more reckless, drank more, swore more, and picked up two or three girls at a time. They got into brawls more often.

IT WAS TO the offshore category that Chet Williams used to belong, but he'd had trouble and was living in one of the upstairs rooms at Pat's Bar, accumulating a huge tab that even Pat was not sure he would ever be able to pay. Recalling that he had been one of her best customers when the going was good, she told her barman to keep giving him beer. She believed that Chet's luck would turn. Some customers had been heard to describe Chet Williams as a disgrace to America, but the other Americans who came to the bar still bought him drinks and considered him merely unlucky. Chet had been like them; he worked for an oil company as a rig engineer and only came to Pat's Bar when he was off duty. Generous and always laughing, he was thin and wiry, and three lines appeared at the corners of his eyes whenever he smiled. Some of the old-timers still recalled how he had once walked up to the stage when Kenny Rogers Junior was singing, taken his guitar and microphone, and belted out "I Can't Get No Satisfaction" to big applause. Pat called him "Engineer Double" because he would always leave the bar with two girls each night after drinking. It was never one girl, and he never went back to the same set of girls twice. The expatriate oil workers said that any problem that Pat could not solve was unsolvable. Pat had gotten Chet Williams out of trouble in the past. He had picked up a girl in a nightclub but did not know that the girl was a Mamiwata, a mermaid. He had such a great time with her and was so grateful the next morning that he gave her a hundred-dollar note, twice the usual amount. But the girl turned down the money and left. The side of the bed on which the girl had slept was wet, as if someone had poured a bucket of water on it. Probably sweat, he assumed, and left for the rig. When he got to the rig, he could not focus on the job he had to do; his mind kept going back to the girl he had slept with. He recalled her contortions and how she kept calling him "my husband, oh my husband." He found himself with a huge erection, his face covered in sweat. He asked for compassionate leave and ran back to Port Harcourt to look for the lady. He went from one nightclub to another, distraught, his eyes wild, asking for Helen, the name she had given him. When he wandered into Pat's Bar screaming her name, Pat could immediately tell what had happened.

"Mr. Chet don fuck Mamiwata be dat o, he no fit sleep again and na Mamiwata him dey see for dream every night wey him sleep."

She took him to a native doctor in Diobu, a suburb in downtown Port Harcourt. The native doctor demanded five thousand naira, a white cock, and a bottle of Seaman's Aromatic Schnapps. He spat some of the schnapps into Chet Williams's eyes, and suddenly the man gripped Pat's arm and, looking around, asked, "Where am I?" He felt as if he had been in a dream all that time, he said.

But Pat had declared Chet Williams's recent troubles unsolvable; in fact, she told some of the expatriates that his best bet was to return to America and start a new life. His recent troubles were caused by girls too. He had picked up two girls from another bar.

The girls claimed to be students at the University of Port Harcourt. Chet Williams had convinced them to do nude shots of themselves and him with his digital camera. When Chet woke up the next morning, the girls had disappeared with his money bag, his cell phone, his Rolex wristwatch, and his gold wrist chain, but had for some reason overlooked the digital camera. He cursed out loud, calling all Nigerian girls prostitutes and thieves. Pat assured him that she would help him catch the girls, but he was not interested. He posted the nude pictures of the girls in an expatriate Web site, Najamericans Online. When the girls heard that he had splashed their nude pictures on the Web, they told the local gossip magazines about Chet Williams and his weird sexual habits. They said they were no thieves; they had stolen his money because he refused to pay them for the nude shots. The newspapers had a field day with the story, splashing the girls' naked pictures on their front page, mentioning Mr. Chet Williams by name, and calling on his employer, a major oil company, to sack him. The papers asked if he would have dared to take pictures of American call girls in his native country without paying them. The oil companies avoided anything that would draw the ire of their host communities; first Chet's employers suspended him, then they fired him. Since then he had been hanging around, hoping to get another job and living at Pat's Bar. But the oil companies operated according to some unwritten rules of cooperation.

The only case that came close to Chet's involved a brash, cursing, beer-bellied Texan called Red Rick. He had gotten into an argument with one of the Nigerian engineers in the rig for not carrying out his instructions properly, and in a fit of rage had called the Nigerian engineer an "educated monkey."

The Nigerian workers in the rig had thrown down their tools and attempted to throw Red Rick into the ocean, but were stopped by the Atlas guards on duty. The story had gotten into the newspapers, and the Nigerian Union of Petroleum and Natural Gas Workers had stepped in and insisted that Rick must be sacked and deported. The newspapers had blown the whole thing out of proportion and actually insisted that there was a tradition of racism among foreign oil workers. No one listened to the argument that it was usual for the oil workers to refer to the Nigerian workers on the rig as monkeys, and for the local workers to refer to the white workers as "oyibo pepper," referring both to the pale color of the white man's skin and his inability to eat peppers. Red Rick hung around in Pat's Bar for a long time while the case was being investigated. Finally, the oil company sacked him and asked him to leave.

ALL THESE WERE small issues compared to the abductions of expatriate oil workers that began to take place at the beginning of the new year in Port Harcourt. There had been abductions in other oil-producing towns with expatriate communities like Warri and Ughelli, but Port Harcourt, fondly called the Garden City, had seemed immune. When the news first filtered in that six foreign oil workers, including two Americans, had been abducted by a group known as the Niger Delta Force, fear gripped the expatriate community. They were used to threats and work stoppage from their host communities, but not armed abductions.

Pat moved from one drinking table to the next.

"No be serious matter at all, at all, the governor don step into the case, even the president, sef, and all the chiefs and royal fathers and soja don full everywhere, no wahala at all, everything is under control."

"What do they want, is it money?"

"Are they connected to any Muslim group? They say their leader has a Muslim name."

"Are Americans their target, or are they after every white person living in Port Harcourt?"

The first of the hostages were set free after a week. They

had only good words for their captors; they said they were very polite young men and were only asking for representation and development for their people. But that first abduction opened a floodgate in the Niger Delta. The news leaked out that the first kidnappers had been paid off handsomely—in foreign currency too—by the oil companies, who had established a ransom fund. This was all the news the unemployed young men in the Niger Delta needed.

The abductors drove up to Pat's Bar in a navy blue Nissan bus in a cloud of dust. They shot sporadically into the air. One of them leaned out of the front passenger seat; he had a red bandanna around his head and military fatigues.

"Lie down, everybody—if you move we shoot you, if you talk we shoot you dead, bring out your cell phones and keep them on the table, if you move, we waste you."

The rest of the abductors jumped out of the bus; they too were dressed in military fatigues and carried AK-47 rifles. They were all barking out orders at the same time. There was dust, smoke, and confusion in the small bar. Some of the expatriates were hiding under the tables. The girls were lying on top of them, shielding them with their bodies.

Pat came out from the kitchen, where she had been supervising one of the cooks who was preparing steak for a customer and began to scream, "What police station are you people from, and who sent you? Don't you know that this is a decent place where oyibo people come to relax, oya, oya, who is your leader, come and see me quick." She had mistaken the abductors for idle soldiers on an extortion raid. Soldiers from the Tombra barracks would occasionally raid bars to extort money whenever they were broke, but they rarely came to Pat's Bar.

One of the gunmen shot at her, but their leader pushed his gun to the side, and the bullet ricocheted off a table. Pat screamed and lay down, calling on Amanyanabo, the god of her forefathers, to save her.

"We want the white men, *oya* come out all of you, one by one, and start marching into the vehicle, quick, quick, march into the bus and let's move, we are not wasting time, anybody that disobey we waste the person one time."

It was then Pat realized that these were no soldiers raiding expatriate bars for small extortion money, but abductors who had come on more serious business. The lights in the bar were very dim, powered by the standby generator that had been running all day due to an outage. Pat crawled to where three of her white customers were sitting and shielded them with her body. The only two people who walked into the waiting bus were an American who worked for Chevron named Pete and Chet Williams. Chet had been sitting alone before the abductors came, nursing a beer and waiting for an opportune moment to ask the barman to bring him three shots of Monkey Tail. He had been playing his favorite mind game to amuse himself, which he called "Why This Country Is Fucked Up."

As long as they continue to have only one kind of doughnut, this country will remain fucked up.

As long as they don't celebrate Thanksgiving, this country will remain fucked up.

As long as they call every kind of pasta macaroni, this country will remain fucked up.

As long as Happy Cow cheese remains the only brand to be found in the country, and even that is hawked in the hot sun, this country will remain fucked up.

As long as they continue to throw tires round the necks of armed robbers, douse them with petrol, and set them ablaze instead of trying them in courts of law, this country will remain fucked up. . . .

He was still enjoying his game when a gun was pointed at his head and he was led away.

The girls knew Chet Williams's story; they knew he had no money, and they stayed away from him. The other American who was abducted, Pete, was a fat, unhappy fellow. He usually wore Levi's and a New York Yankees baseball cap, preferred young boys, and always looked sullen, which made the girls stay away from him as well.

As the bus pulled away, the abductors shot into the air and shouted, "You will hear from us." People began to stand up from the floor; two of the expatriates had urinated on themselves, and they pointed at each other and laughed nervously. They emptied their wallets, giving all the money in them to the girls who had shielded them, fled into their cars, and sped off.

The news soon spread that two Americans had been abducted from Pat's Bar, and the story made the local newspapers. The governor of the state invited Pat and whoever had been at the bar to come forward and debrief the security operatives. He called on the oil companies not to pay ransom money to anybody.

THE ABDUCTORS CALLED themselves names like Rambo, 007, Chuck Norris, and Hulk Hogan. They were all very dark-complexioned and were visibly excited, like fishermen celebrating a big catch. As they drove the bus at high speed through the streets of Port Harcourt, Chet prayed that they would run into a police checkpoint. Pete was crying, big tears running down his face and snot down his nose; he looked too scared to wipe off the snot. Surprisingly, there were no police checkpoints on the road that night. Ordinarily, every quarter mile featured a point where the policemen would ask for bribes. If they noticed that the car was carrying a white person, their manner immediately turned servile. "Oga oyibo your boys are here working for you, abeg find your boys something to do the weekend, as you can see we are here protecting you, nothing is too small, any small thing is appreciated even if na dollar or pound sterling." Tonight the policemen were nowhere to be found.

The bus was headed toward the outskirts of Port Harcourt; Chet could tell that they were leaving Port Harcourt because the smell of flaring gas that suffused the city was beginning to fade.

Pete turned to Chet and began to whisper, barely audible because of the snot and tears that choked his voice.

"What are they gonna do with us, you think they're gonna kill us, man?"

"Why would they wanna kill us? If they kill us, they will not be able to collect any ransom."

"Hey sharrap there, the two both of you," Rambo screamed at them.

"Leave them let them talk, Rambo, if they want to nack tori let dem nack, no wahala afterall we don get wetin we want and na make pay drop na him remain, make you no make dem begin fear and come get heart attack and die."

Turning to Pete and Chet, Rambo smiled, showing a set of very large but perfectly white teeth.

"Make una no fear, make una dey nack tori dey go, no wahala, we are all together."

The bus turned off the highway and entered a bumpy dirt road. The leaves of the plants that grew along the narrow road slapped against the side of the bus. Pete rested his head on the seat in front of him and began to sob, his shoulders quaking.

They soon arrived at a small beach. Rambo and 007 jumped down into the surrounding bush, dragged out a boat on which was mounted an Evinrude outboard engine, and pulled the boat to the edge of the water.

"Get into the boat quick, time waits for no man, let's move abeg no killing of time we don already waste time for Port Harcourt make we they move, oya, oya."

They got into the boat. Though Pete was used to boats, since he worked on an offshore rig, he looked at the water strangely, as if he was seeing water for the first time, and entered the boat with shaky legs.

"CAN YOU IMAGINE, they are asking for ten million naira each for Chet and Pete? They say the community relations manager in Pete's office don dey negotiate with dem. But na who go come negotiate for Chet now? Eeehen, tell me, man wey get wahala wey no get work infact na book me down him de take live for this my bar."

The few expatriates who were around looked at Pat and stared back into their mugs of beer.

"I hear Pete will soon be released—the community relations guy in his office was seen picking up unmarked notes from

Savannah Bank," one of the expatriates said to no one in particular and went back to his beer.

"So what will happen to Chet? Who is going to help the cow with no tail to drive away flies?" Pat said and walked away, shaking her head.

There were few girls in the bar. They only came early in the evening to check out the place and then move on to other bars with more life. Even the expatriates were beginning to avoid the place. Some of them were already referring to the place as "bad luck bar." This did not bother Pat much; she had seen it all. She consoled herself with something she always heard her mother say in times of difficulty. According to her mother, the bedbug once remarked to her children that whatever was hot would soon get cold. This was after an old woman on whose old wooden bed the bedbugs had made their home poured hot water on the bed to get rid of them.

CHET WAS PLAYING his favorite game again.

As long as these people continue to sell water in plastic bags and peanuts in bottles, this country will remain fucked up.

As long as the roads here continue to be built without sidewalks and motorists continue to struggle for road space with pedestrians, beggars, hawkers, and cows, this country will remain fucked up.

As long as the electric company refuses to supply power and the entire country runs on generators, yet no one thinks it wise to shut down the power company, this country will remain fucked up.

As long as it remains easier to buy petrol from the black market and the filling stations are choked with long lines of motorists even though the country is one of the largest exporters of crude oil, this country will remain fucked up.

As long as there are more mosquitoes than human beings, this country will remain fucked up.

Rambo's voice cut into his thoughts; this made him a little angry, as he was enjoying the game. He could sometimes get to seventy reasons before he stopped. Rambo and his friends had treated them well. They provided bottled water and Off! mosquito repellent. They provided a tent for them and even offered Chet marijuana and schnapps. The only downside was that each time either he or Pete needed to shit, he had to do it in the brackish waters of the mangrove. He had heard the expression "nervous wreck," but only thought it a figure of speech until his abduction with Pete, who was either crying or shitting or pissing or asking him if they were going to be killed or cowering in a corner.

"Mr. Chet, your people have refused to perform o, nobody is responding concerning your own matter o. Mr. Pete's people have responded very well, in fact we are going to release him as soon as my people come back."

"Who are my people? I have no people."

"I mean your company people, or are you not working in an oil company?"

"I lied—I no longer work for Atlas Oil, I was laid off months ago."

"You mean you are not working for Atlas? Elelele, Hulk Hogan, everybody please come o, we have bought bad market o . . ."

Rambo's colleagues crowded around him and began to fire rapid questions at him.

"So who are you working for now?"

"I have no job. I already told your leader, I lost my job months back, and I'm trying to get another job."

"That is a big lie, we have never heard of a white person in this Port Harcourt who has no job."

"Well, you are meeting the first one, congratulations," Chet said, laughing recklessly.

From where Pete sat, he could hear the conversation, but each time Chet looked at him, he quickly looked away.

"But you can call your people—I mean, other white people like you, oyibos like to help each other, they can contribute money for you to be released."

"I told you before, I have nobody," Chet said.

A few days later, Pete's employers paid up. Rambo and his colleagues drank and danced and celebrated, throwing money into the air and pasting currency notes on each other's sweaty faces.

Later that day, they packed and left with Pete in their boat. They left Chet behind. He was almost tempted to doze, but he remembered his game, became suddenly alert, and began to play.

As long as abducting foreigners continues to pay good money and the young people of this country remain unemployed. . . .

When it began to grow dark, Chet Williams began to feel a bit hungry. He was looking forward to the darkness and time alone with the stars. He always felt a particular kinship with the Southern Cross. The sky over here always felt very close, and when it grew dark, it was the color of dark blue ink. Someone had once told him that the sky was close in Nigeria because the people were not greedy. The person told him that when the world was first created, the sky was so close, and the sky was edible.

All you had to do was reach up and cut a piece and eat. The only rule was that you could only cut the quantity you needed to fill you, none should be left overnight. Unfortunately, in some parts of the world people became greedy and began to cut more than they needed, and the sky began to flee upward. He told Chet that the sky was farthest where the people were greediest.

Chet looked up again and saw a distant faint glow. That must be the glow of the gas flare from Port Harcourt Refinery, he told himself. He stood up and began to follow it.

Pilgrimage

I liked her before I met her. She had a short name—Beth, this was easy for me to write on the placard I had to hold up at the arrival hall. She was also American, which meant her tips were going to be large. I had trouble with some of the names; just last week there was a couple with a Laotian name, though they were Canadians—Phonprompasang, I think, was their name. They said I spelled it wrong, and that set the tone of our relationship all through their visit. It was the wife who observed the error in my spelling. The man was too ill to observe anything; he was sweating through his short-sleeved white shirt, and by the time they entered my bus, he was fast asleep. I am not any kind of expert; I am only a driver for the Temple of All Nations.

My job is to pick up foreigners from every part of the world who began flocking to the temple for healing after the prophet's tour of fifteen world capitals. I was surprised at the number of people that I had to pick up every day—Americans, Canadians, Australians, South Africans, Norwegians, Swedes, in fact, people from almost every country on earth. And the kinds of sicknesses they suffered from, even things I have never heard of before—cancers of every part of the body, paralysis of the mouth, ear, nose, eye, some things we do not even consider a sickness, like restless leg syndrome, they flew thousands of miles to find a cure for them here in the temple.

I was shocked when she walked toward me. She was black like me—well, not as black, but she was not white. She had a plump, smooth face; her hair was in braids like some of our women's. She was dressed in a light green *bubu*, and if she had walked by me on the street I could have mistaken her for some rich man's wife. She stretched out her hand, but I took her bag instead. I made to pick up the rest of her luggage, but she stopped me.

"We should at least get introduced—I am Beth, Beth Morgan," she said.

"I am Augustine, I work for the Temple of All Nations, I am your driver."

"That's awesome," she said. "Let's go. This heat is killing me."

I gathered up her things, and we began to wade through the thick throng of touts, policemen, customs and excise officers, men of the air force, police, and navy, pickpockets, con men, travelers, and a few people who had come to welcome their friends and relations from overseas. I was watching her; she took in everything like a child before a large cinema screen. When she spoke to me earlier, I had realized that though she was black, there was no difference between the way she and the other white Americans who had visited the temple spoke.

When we got to where the minivan was parked, I put away her luggage and told her to sit in the back seat, but she opened the passenger seat in front and took the seat beside mine. I noticed that she was doing well under the heat; some of our visitors

would have turned the color of ripe tomatoes between the arrival hall and the car park. We pulled out of the car park and
joined Airport Road toward the temple. I turned on the air conditioner and the radio, but she turned them off. I apologized.
We eased into heavy traffic, and soon it came to a crawl. We
were surrounded by hawkers, selling everything from car stereos
to standing fans, bread, bottled water, oil paintings, cigarettes,
chewing gum, and ice water in cellophane bags. I cursed under
my breath as the hawkers swarmed the vehicle. I was ashamed;
this was why I had wanted the air conditioner turned on. The
hawkers thrust different items into her face, screaming, *Buy,
buy, buy, buy, buy,* like angry bees. I screamed at them to move
away from the car, but she was laughing. Can you imagine that?
She was laughing.

"Who are these people, why are they on the street?" she
asked.

"Hawkers, beggars, and thieves. They are watching for a
careless moment to snatch your bag or cut your necklace from
your neck."

I had added the last bit to scare her. Though it was true that
some bold thieves would cut jewelry from commuters' necks and
ears, this rarely happened. But she was apparently not scared, as
she made no effort to wind up the glass on her side of the car.
The traffic was moving again, and I was grateful. I wanted to get
her to the temple as early as possible so she could have some rest
and be ready for the miracle service, which was what she'd come
for that evening.

The traffic slowed down to a crawl once more. We were at a
road junction this time. I stepped gently on the brakes as a woman
in a flowery, light blue cotton *iro* and *buba* came toward us. She

was carrying a pair of twins, one male, one female, on either arm. The male's clean-shaven head was dripping with sweat, and the mother was wiping it with her wrists. She stretched out her hands to my passenger, asking for money. She turned to me.

"Why is she begging? There is apparently nothing the matter with her, at least nothing that I can see."

"She is a mother of twins, and according to her culture, she has to beg for forty days or her twins will die. She has to disgrace herself for her good fortune to prove to the gods and to those who have no children that she deserves the twins."

"Oh, I see," she said. The beggar woman moved away. My passenger closed her eyes, lost in thought. She was different, this one, I said to myself. Other foreign guests would usually deluge me with questions about the prophet and his healing powers. At this point, I would have known what disease they were seeking a cure from, but she had not told me anything. She acted more like a tourist than a pilgrim. I figured this was because she was a black American, and this had once been her land. I did not much bother myself with these thoughts. The members of the welcome committee would be getting impatient by now. A man carrying over two dozen dried rats of different sizes suddenly thrust two smelly dead dry rats at Beth through the open window and screamed "Kill rat! Kill rat! Dry and kill!" The car was filled with the smell of dead rats. I screamed at him to get his smelly wares out of my car. I looked at my passenger. She had an amused look on her face. She wanted to know who the man was; I responded that he was a seller of rat traps and rat poison, and wore the dead rats around his neck to show how effective his wares were.

Suddenly, there was the sound of running feet like the

stampede of a thousand horses. The roadside hawkers were fleeing into the surrounding streets, as soldiers with *koboko* horsewhips and guns kicked, punched, and hit with the butts of their
guns all those who could not run away quickly enough. They
tossed both people and goods into their open truck; the people
were screaming and crying. One of the soldiers was setting fire
to some of the items that the fleeing hawkers had abandoned in
their fight. My passenger was gripping my arms tightly; the traffic had started to move.

"What is going on?" she asked.

"The soldiers are members of the Task Force on Street Trading. They raid the hawkers weekly and seize their goods, but
the hawkers will get their goods back after giving bribes to their
bosses. And the next day, they are back on the street."

"And the government, what is the government doing?"

"They were sent by the government—the government set up
the task force."

"I mean, why don't they build shops for the traders?"

"The shops are too expensive. The government sells the shops
to middlemen who resell to the traders at a highly inflated price,
and most of the traders can't afford the rent for the shops."

My passenger appeared to be lost in thought, and soon we
were at the Temple of All Nations. The members of the welcome
committee came, ushered my passenger out of the car, and took
her to her lodgings. The temple had built special lodgings with
showers, well-furnished bedrooms, and constant electric supply
for the guests who came from overseas—something close to the
level of comfort they were used to in their home countries.

It still amazes me how the temple had grown, from a few
worshippers who sat on wooden benches singing and clapping

under a tree on Sunday mornings to hundreds of thousands of worshippers from every part of the world. But then again, it was not so difficult. The prophet had always told those of us who started out with him that we were privileged, because one day soon he would become the property of the whole world. I think the big growth came after the visit to the temple by that president from one of the southern African countries. Some say he came to seek the prophet's prayers to win his tenth election. Others said he had a strange illness that could not be cured by even the best Western doctors. He came to the prophet without his guards, dressed in a simple light brown shirt and black trousers. He knelt before the prophet, and as the prophet laid hands on him, he began to shed tears like a baby. His tear-drenched face was all over the newspapers the next day. He won the elections, of course, and bought the prophet a private jet and built the temple.

We, the members of the temple, do not wear shoes, and we are always dressed in white as a sign of our holiness.

The healing service that night had hundreds of thousands of people from every part of the world in attendance. The auditorium was filled with so many people dressed in white, waving their white handkerchiefs in the air, the choir singing and drumming forcefully. Some of the worshippers placed their bottles of olive oil for healing beside the huge loudspeakers that were mounted on the walls. At some point, as the choir sang, a voice would scream out, and the ushers would rush to gather a falling human form in their arms. As the prophet mounted the podium, there was shouting and waving of white handkerchiefs. He stretched out his hands; people in the direction in which his hands spread out were falling and screaming and babbling. By the time he finished the healing service, thousands had come forth to testify that they had been healed. The foreigners among them were filmed for the temple's television program. I went over to Beth's room after the service. She looked a bit tired. I could not ask her if she had been healed. She told me to come and take her out shopping and sightseeing the next day.

IT RAINED THAT morning, and Oyingbo Market was wet and slippery. We had to step gingerly between the stalls. I was taking Beth to the part of the market where I usually took foreigners, where they sold textiles, woodcarvings, and locally made necklaces, when she began pointing at some stalls toward the rear of the market. This was the area of the market where dried herbs, herbal concoctions, skulls of monkeys and other animals, and even human skulls were sold. I told her that there was nothing that would interest her there, but she insisted that we go in that direction.

We stopped before an old woman in one of the stalls. A strong smell of herbs and dried animals emanated from her; she was dark-complexioned and had three tribal scars on each side of her face.

"My daughter, you have come from a far place, and yet you have come back home," she said to Beth, reaching out to her and holding her palms in her own dark, wrinkled hands. Beth smiled.

"You were taken away, screaming and cursing, but you promised to return. You have a lump under your left breast, and all the white man's medicine could not cure you; you have journeyed well, and now you can return in peace."

I wanted to drag Beth away before the old woman trapped her even further with her magic, but she was smiling, and yet she had tears in her eyes. The old woman removed her head tie and began to tie it around Beth's head, all the while calling on the other women to come and join her in welcoming a lost daughter who had returned after crossing many seas and oceans. From the surrounding stalls, women began to emerge, clapping and singing, their voices ringing through the din of the market. I stood aside like a spectator, hoping that no one from the temple would see us. They were touching Beth all over her body, examining her the way doctors examine a newborn baby, and all the while she was smiling, with tears running down her face. One of the women rushed to her shop and came back with a white egg and a calabash. She threw the egg at Beth, and it shattered, the egg yolk wetting and running down her clothes. They grabbed her face, made three quick incisions on her forehead, and rubbed a dark, powdery substance from the calabash on it.

The women went back to their stalls and came back with gifts—clothes, herbs, head ties, necklaces, wooden dolls. They piled the gifts in front of her. She put her hands in her purse to give them money, but they looked offended. Just as they came, they left, chattering excitedly among themselves like black birds. Beth was touching herself under her breast and saying breathlessly, "It is gone, it is gone."

"It was never there, my daughter," the old woman said.

I WAS TAKING Beth to the airport for her flight back to the United States. She was looking straight ahead. We passed a one-armed, one-eyed beggar turned impromptu traffic warden who was directing the traffic that was quickly building up. Meanwhile, the traffic policemen were sitting under a thatched shed down the road drinking *ogogoro*, smoking cigarettes, and chatting idly. She turned toward me and began to speak.

"I felt the lump for the first time one morning after my fifty-fifth birthday. It was scary. A couple of my friends had had cancer. One of them had died from it. I kept touching myself on the way to the school where I was a teacher. I called my doctor and made an appointment."

She paused and was silent. Commercial bus drivers were giving money to the emergency traffic warden; I heard a few of them praising him and saying other beggars should emulate him and look for something to do instead of begging on the streets.

"But the doctors could not find anything. All the X-rays, all the scans, blood tests, urine tests—they came up with nothing. I was beginning to suspect that the people at the hospital were whispering behind my back. My doctor even suggested I see an analyst. And then I saw the prophet on television. I decided that he might be able to heal me after I saw the pile of wheelchairs on the stage, left behind by those who claimed he had healed them. And besides, I had always dreamed of visiting Africa. At the healing service last night, the lump was still there. I wondered if the trip had been in vain, and then at the market when that old woman touched me, I felt lighter, as if a large moth had flown out from under my breast. In your car I touched myself just to be sure."

Traffic was moving again, and we were soon at the departure hall. I helped her with her bag—this used to be my moment—but when she stretched out her hand and extended several dollar bills to me, I shook my head. She extended both hands and hugged me, and walked away to catch her flight.

Voice of America

We were sitting in front of Ambo's provision store, drinking the local gin, *ogogoro*, mixed with Coke and listening to a program called *Music Time in Africa* on the Voice of America. We were mostly young men who were spending our long summer holidays in the village. Some of us whose parents were too poor to pay our school fees spent the long vacation doing odd jobs in the village so we could save money to pay our school fees. Someone remarked on how clear the broadcast was, compared to our local radio broadcasts, which were filled with static. The presenter announced that there was a special request for an African song from an American girl whose name was Laura Williams, and that she was also interested in pen pals from every part of Africa, especially Nigeria. Onwordi, who had been pensive all this while, rushed to Ambo the shopkeeper, collected a pen, and began to take down her address. This immediately led to a scramble among the rest of us to get the address too. We all took it down, folded the pieces of paper, put them in our pockets, and promised we were going to write as soon as we got home that night.

A debate soon ensued among us concerning the girl who wanted pen pals from Africa.

"Before our letter gets to her, she will have received thousands from the city boys who live in Lagos and will throw our letters into the trash can," Dennis said.

"Yes, you may be right," remarked Sunday, "and besides, even if she writes you, you may not have anything in common to share. But the boys who live in the city go to nightclubs and know the lyrics of the latest songs by Michael Jackson and Dynasty. They are the ones who see the latest movies, not the dead Chinese kung fu and Sonny Chiba films that Fantasia Cinema screens for us in the village once every month."

"But you can never tell with these Americans—she could be interested in being friends with a real village boy because she lives in the big city herself and is probably tired of city boys." Lucky, who said this, was the oldest among us and had spent three years repeating form four.

"I once met an American lady in Onitsha where I went to buy goods for my shop," Ambo the shopkeeper said. He hardly spoke to us, only listening and smiling and looking at the figures in his *Daily Reckoner.*

We all turned to Ambo in surprise. We knew that he traveled to the famous Onitsha Market, the biggest market in West Africa, to buy goods every week; we could hardly believe that he had met an American lady. Onitsha Market was said to be so big that half of those who came there to buy and sell were not humans but spirits. It was said that a simple way of knowing the spirits when in the market was to bend down and look through your legs at the feet of people walking through. If you looked well and closely enough, you would notice some walkers whose soles did not quite touch the ground. These were the spirits. If they got a good bargain from a trader, he would discover that the money in his money box miraculously grew every day, but any trader who cheated them would find his money disappearing from his money box without any rational explanation.

"She was wearing an ordinary Ankara skirt and a blouse made from local fabrics, and had come to buy a leather purse and hat from the Hausa traders. She even exchanged a few words in Hausa with the traders. The way she said 'ina kwu ana nkwu' was so sweet and melodious, it was like listening to a canary singing."

"She was probably a volunteer schoolteacher in one of the girls' secondary schools around Onitsha, and has lived here for so long she does not count as an American. We are talking of a real American girl living on American soil." Jekwu, who said this, was Ambo's adversary as a result of a dispute over an old debt and was permanently on the opposite side of any argument with Ambo.

"Well, what I was trying to say was that she might be interested in a village boy. Like the one I saw in Onitsha, who was wearing a local dress and spoke Hausa, I am sure she will be interested in a village boy," Ambo said and went back to his *Daily Reckoner.*

Someone ordered another round of *ogogoro* and Coke, and we all began to drink and became silent as we thought our own thoughts. The moon dipped, and everywhere suddenly became dark. One by one we rose and left for our homes.

. . . .

WE WERE SITTING in Ambo's shop one evening when Onwordi swaggered in holding a white envelope with a small American stamp. There was a bald eagle on the stamp. He waved it in our faces, smiling. He called for drinks, and we all rushed to him, trying to snatch the envelope from his hands.

"She has replied," he said, looking very proud, like a man who had unexpectedly caught a big fish with a hook in the small village river. The truth was that we had all forgotten about the announcement on the radio program, and I had actually washed the shorts in whose back pocket I put the paper where I jotted down the address.

Onwordi began to read from the letter. The girl's name was Laura Williams. She had recently moved with her parents to a farm in Iowa from a much larger city. She had one more year before finishing high school. She was going to take a class called "Africa: Its People and Culture" in the fall and was curious to know more about African culture. She wanted to know whether Onwordi lived in the city or in a village. She also wanted to know if he lived close to lots of wild animals like giraffes, lions, and chimpanzees. And what kind of food did he generally eat, was it spicy? And how was it prepared? She also wanted to know if he came from a large family. She ended the letter with the phrase "Yours, Laura."

"Oh, my God," Lucky said, "this is a love letter. The American lady is searching for an African husband."

"Why do you say that?" Onwordi said, clearly very excited about such a prospect. Though he had read the letter over a hundred times and was hoping for such a stroke of good fortune, he had not seen any hint of it in the letter.

"See the way she ended the letter? She was practically telling you that she is yours from now on."

"I think that is the American way of ending letters," Dennis said. He was the most well-read among us, having read the entire oeuvre of James Hadley Chase and Nick Carter. He used big words and would occasionally refer to some girl in the village as a "doll" or some other as a "deadbeat floozy."

"But that is not even the main issue; she can become your girlfriend in due course if you know how to play your game very well. You could tell her that you have a giraffe farm, and that you ride on the back of a tiger to your farm," he continued.

"But she is soon going to ask for your photograph, and you know we have no giraffes here and the last we heard of a lion was when one was said to have been sighted by a hunter well over ten years ago," Jekwu said. "You should ask her to send you a ten-dollar bill, tell her you want to see what it looks like, and when she sends it, we can change it in the black market at Onitsha for one thousand naira and use the money for *ogogoro*." Jekwu took a drink and wiped his eyes, which were misting over from the drink.

"If you ask her for money, you are going to scare her away. White women are interested in love and romance. Write her a letter professing your love for her and asking for her hand in marriage—tell her that you would love to come and join her in America, and see what she has to say to that," Dennis said.

"Promise her you'll send her some records by Rex Jim Lawson if she can send you 'Do Me Right Baby,' " Lucky added.

"A guy in my school once had a female pen pal from India. She would ask him to place her letters under his pillow when he slept. At night she would appear in his dreams and make love to him. He said he always woke up in the mornings exhausted and worn out after the marathon lovemaking sessions in the dreams.

We do not know how it happened, but he later found out the girl had died years back."

We were all shocked into silence by Dennis's story. Ambo turned up the volume of the radio, and we began to listen to the news in special English. The war in Palestine was progressing apace, blacks in South Africa were still rioting in Soweto, and children were dying of hunger in Ethiopia and Eritrea.

Onwordi said nothing. He smiled at our comments, holding the letter close to his chest somehow like hugging a lover. He thanked us for our suggestions and was the first to leave Ambo's shop that night.

TWO WEEKS LATER, Onwordi walked into the shop again, smiling and holding an envelope with an American flag stamp close to his chest once more. We circled him and began to ask him questions. She had written once again. She thanked him for his mail. She was glad to know he lived in a village. She was interested in knowing what life was like in a typical African village. What kind of house did he live in, how did he get his drinking water? What kind of school did he attend, and how had he learned to write in English? She said she would love to see his photograph, though she did not have any of hers that she could share with him at the present time. Postal regulations would not permit her to send money by mail, but she could take a picture of a ten-dollar bill and send it to him if all he really wanted was to see what it looked like. She also said she was interested in knowing about African talking drums—did they really talk? She said she looked forward to hearing from him again. We were silent as we listened to him, and then we all began to speak at once.

"I was right about her being interested in you; otherwise why would she request for your picture without sending you hers?"

"This shows that women all over the world are coy. She was only being cunning. She really wants to know what you look like before she gets involved with you."

"You should go and borrow a suit from the schoolteacher and go to Sim Paul's Photo Studio in the morning when he is not yet drunk and let him take a nice shot of you so you can send it to her."

"How about you borrow the schoolteacher's suit and Ambo's shirt and Dennis's black school tie and Lucky's silk flower-patterned shirt and Sim Paul's shoes and tell the schoolteacher's wife to lend you her stretching comb to straighten your hair if you can't afford Wellastrate cream; then you'll be like the most handsome suitor in the folktale."

"Who is the most handsome suitor?" Onwordi asked. "I have never heard that folktale." Jekwu cleared his throat, took a sip from his *ogogoro* and Coke, and began his story.

"Once in the land of Idunoba there lived a girl who was the prettiest girl in the entire kingdom. Her beauty shone like the sun, and her teeth glittered like pearls whenever she smiled. All the young men in the kingdom asked for her hand in marriage, but she turned them down. She turned down the men either because they were too tall or too short or too hairy or not hairy enough. She said that since she was the most beautiful girl in the kingdom, she could only marry the most handsome man. Her fame soon got to the land of the spirits, and the most wicked spirit of them all, Tongo, heard about her and said he was going to marry her. Not only was Tongo the most wicked, he was also the most ugly, possessing only a cracked skull for a head. He was all bones, and when he walked, his bones rattled. Before setting out to ask for the hand of the maiden in marriage, Tongo went round the land of the spirits to borrow body parts. From the spirit with the straightest pair of legs, he borrowed a straight pair of legs, and from the one with the best skin, he borrowed a smooth and glowing skin. He went round borrowing body parts until he was transformed into the most handsome man there was. As soon as he walked into Idu on market day and the maiden set eyes on him, she began following him around until he turned, smiled at her, and asked for her hand in marriage. She took him to her parents and hurriedly packed her things, waved them good-bye, and followed the handsome suitor.

On their way to his home, which was across seven rivers and seven hills, she was so busy admiring his handsomeness that she did not grow tired and was not bothered by the fact that they were leaving all the human habitations behind. It was only when they crossed into the land of the spirits, and he walked into the first house and came out crooked because he had returned the straight legs to their owner, that she began to sense that something was wrong. And so she continued to watch as he returned the skin, the arms, the hair, and the other borrowed body parts, so that by the time they got to his house, only his skull was left. She wept when she realized she had married an ugly spirit, but she knew it was too late to return to the land of the living, so she bided her time. When Tongo approached her for lovemaking, she told him to go and borrow all the body parts he had on when he married her. Because Tongo loved her headstrong nature, he agreed. Each time they made love, he went round borrowing body parts, and when they had a child, the child was a very handsome child and grew into the most handsome man."

We all laughed at the story and advised Onwordi to work at transforming himself into the most handsome man. Ambo advised him to dress in traditional African clothes as, from what he knew about white people, this was likely to appeal to her more.

"So what are you going to do?" we asked Onwordi, but he only smiled and held his letter tightly as he drank.

The next time *Music Time in Africa* was on the air, we had our pens ready to take down the names of pen pals, but the few that were announced were listeners from other parts of Africa, and we all felt disappointed.

We waited for Onwordi to walk in with a letter, but he did not for quite some time. We wondered what had happened. When he finally walked in after some days, he looked dejected and would not say a word to any of us.

"Hope you have not upset her with your last mail?" Lucky said. "You know white people are very sensitive, and you may have hurt her feelings without knowing it."

"This is why we told you to always let us see the letter before you send it to her. When we put our heads together and craft a letter to her, she will pack her things and move into your house, leaking roof and all. As the elders say, when you piss on one spot, it is more likely to froth."

"But exactly what did you write to her that has made her silent?" Lucky asked. Onwordi was silent, but he smiled liked a dumb man who has accidentally glimpsed a young woman's pointed breast and ordered more drinks. "Or have you started hiding her mail from us? Maybe the contents are too intimate for our eyes. Or now that you have become closer, has she started kissing her letters with lipstick-painted lips and sealing the letters with kisses?" Ambo teased. But nothing we said would make Onwordi say a word.

ONWORDI WALKED INTO Ambo's shop after a period of three weeks, holding the envelope that we had become used to by now and looking morose. We all turned to him and began to speak at once.

"What happened—has she confessed that she has a husband, or why are you looking so sad?"

"Has she fallen in love with another man? I hear white women fall out of love as quickly as they fall in love."

"If you have her telephone number, I can take you to the Post and Telegrams Office in Onitsha if you have the money and help you make a call to her," Ambo suggested.

Onwordi opened the envelope and brought out a photograph. We all crowded around him to take a closer look. It was the picture of the American girl Laura Williams. The portrait showed only her face. She had an open friendly face with brown hair and slightly chubby cheeks. She was smiling brightly in the photograph. Our damp fingers were already leaving a smudge on the face.

"She is beautiful and looks really friendly, but why did she not send you a photograph where her legs are showing? That way you do not end up marrying a cripple."

Onwordi was not smiling.

"So what did she say in her letter, or have the contents have become too intimate for you to share with us?"

"She says that this is going to be her last letter to me. She says she's done with her paper, and she did very well and illustrated her paper with some of the things I had told her about African culture. But she says her parents are moving back to the city, that the farm has not worked out as planned. She also said she has become interested in Japanese haiku and is in search of new friends from Japan."

"Is that why you are looking sad, like a dog whose juicy morsel fell on the sand? You should thank God for saving you from a relationship where each time the lady clears her throat, you have to jump. Sit down and drink with us, forget your sorrows, and let the devil be ashamed," Jekwu said.

We all laughed, but Onwordi did not laugh with us; he walked away in a slight daze. From that time onward we never saw him at Ambo's shop again. Some people who went to check in on him said they found him lying on his bed with Laura Williams's letters and picture on his chest as he stared up into the tin roof.